"The past is never dead. It's not even past. All of us labor in webs spun long before we were born, webs of heredity and environment, of desire and consequence, of history and eternity. Haunted by wrong turns and roads not taken, we pursue images perceived as new but whose providence dates to the dim dramas of childhood, which are themselves but ripples of consequence echoing down the generations."

—WILLIAM FAULKNER

Savannah Secrets

Savannah Secrets

Willful Transgressions

KATHLEEN Y'BARBO

Danbury, Connecticut

Worthington Family Tree

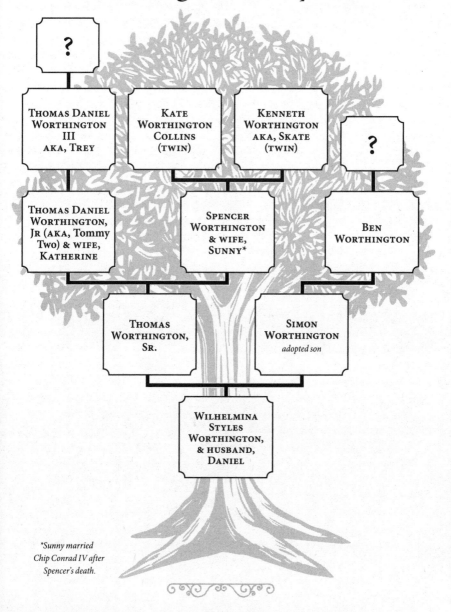

?

THOMAS DANIEL WORTHINGTON III AKA, TREY

KATE WORTHINGTON COLLINS (TWIN)

KENNETH WORTHINGTON AKA, SKATE (TWIN)

?

THOMAS DANIEL WORTHINGTON, JR (AKA, TOMMY TWO) & WIFE, KATHERINE

SPENCER WORTHINGTON & WIFE, SUNNY*

BEN WORTHINGTON

THOMAS WORTHINGTON, SR.

SIMON WORTHINGTON *adopted son*

WILHELMINA STYLES WORTHINGTON, & HUSBAND, DANIEL

Sunny married Chip Conrad IV after Spencer's death.

Chapter One

MEREDITH BELLEFONTAINE SHIFTED IN HER seat and glanced back to see that Julia Foley, her best friend and partner at Magnolia Investigations, was hurrying up the aisle. It wasn't like Julia to be late, especially to a funeral.

"I'm sorry," she said as she settled down on the church pew and tucked a strand of silver hair behind her ear. "I had car trouble. Beau's car is at the airport, so I had to call a ride share. Anyway, I'm glad you saved me a seat. This place is packed."

"Of course it is. Everyone in Savannah knew Tommy Two."

Tommy Two, whose real name was Thomas Daniel Worthington, Jr., was the grandson of Daniel Worthington, a man who owned half of Savannah when he died under mysterious circumstances in 1971. Not literally half, of course, but practically, given the vastness of his real estate holdings and the wealth he had accumulated. Thomas Sr. and his younger brother, Simon, took over the business interests of the Worthington family, but they could never quite manage to control their mother, Wilhelmina.

Now, some sixty years after Wilhelmina Styles Worthington penned her infamous will disinheriting her children and grandchildren from her estate, the clause governing the distribution of the family's millions held in trust and untouchable by any living

Worthington had been satisfied. With the death of Tommy Two, the last known surviving grandchild was dead.

Meredith had known Tommy Two as a rather kind man who lived nearby. She'd been shocked when Trey, or Thomas the Third, Tommy's only son and a University of Georgia graduate, had been indicted in a high-profile case involving organized crime's influence in the New York banking industry. Trey agreed to testify, and that was the last anyone heard of him.

Literally.

Around Savannah, the consensus was that Trey Worthington had disappeared into the witness protection program. Some, however, believed the Mob had the final say in his destination—or rather, resting place. Meredith thought of Thomas III on occasion, especially when Georgia played football, and said a prayer that he was alive and safe, wherever he might be.

She leaned to her right to get a better view of the family pew on the front row. Tommy Two's wife, Katherine, died last year, an event that some say sent Tommy Two careening in the same direction at light speed. He lasted seven months once she was gone, a testament to their long and lasting love.

Tommy Two's younger brother, Spencer, lost his life in a boating accident, leaving behind a young widow, Sunny, and twins Kate and Kenneth. Sunny Worthington Conrad, now married to investment banker Chip Conrad IV, sat between her husband and her pretty blond daughter.

Now married with young children, Kate Worthington Collins was a well-loved weather forecaster for the local television station

WSVG. More than once since Meredith sat down Kate had glanced around the room as if she hoped someone was coming.

Likely her brother, since he was absent from the family pew, Meredith decided. Kenneth, also known as Skate—whose profession was skateboarding, according to the scuttlebutt going around at the beauty shop yesterday. Since the two ladies were the only ones other than Chip Conrad to be seated in the family pew, it appeared Kenneth had decided not to attend today.

Trey was missing as well, but then it would have been a bigger surprise to find him here today.

When the service was over, a who's who of Savannah society exited the church and made their way down the white marble steps of the venerable First Baptist Church to await the slow drive to the Bonaventure Cemetery. The Worthington family had kept a mausoleum under the moss-covered oaks since the turn of the last century.

The first Worthington plopped down a few coins for a substantial piece of land in what became downtown Savannah, but unfortunately he didn't stay alive long enough to enjoy it. With the Worthington family, that was apparently a common thing to do.

After weaving her way around the conversations being held on the steps despite the unseasonably warm and humid November morning, Meredith stopped at the sidewalk to wait for Julia. Why was it that her best friend's hair never danced to the tune of Savannah humidity? While Meredith had spent a full half hour trying to keep her curls from turning to frizz, Julia's silky silver tresses were absolutely unaffected.

Meredith didn't dare take a peek at the mirror in her compact. She knew without looking that the latest round of pricy hair products had been bested by the morning air.

"I'm assuming you'll be riding with me," Meredith said when Julia joined her, reminding herself this was a funeral and not a fashion show.

"That's the plan," Julia replied. "Beau will pick me up from the office later." She paused. "You are going back to the office after the graveside service, aren't you? I know some are invited back to the Worthington home for a reception after, but since I'm not in the inner circle of Savannah society, I wasn't included. Were you?"

Meredith had been but probably because of her proximity as a neighbor rather than any sort of social standing she might have. "I hadn't planned on going," was the answer she chose.

It was the truth. She hadn't.

"Julia, Meredith!"

A glance in the direction of whoever called her name showed a somewhat familiar face coming toward her, Attorney Theophilus Tiberius Lucas III. "Theo Lucas," she said when the young lawyer drew near. "Is that you?"

"It is," he called. "Could I have a word with you two?"

"Of course," Julia said.

"It's good to see you," Meredith added. "I was so sorry to hear of your grandfather's passing. I didn't get to speak to you personally at the funeral."

Meredith had certainly attended more than her fair share of funerals in recent days. Just six weeks ago Theophilus Tiberius Lucas Sr. had opened the back door of Lucas, Wilson, Kyler &

Strong, the law office where he had been the senior partner since 1960, as he habitually did every weekday morning at precisely seven thirty-five. Theo Sr. had taken a seat behind the massive desk in his grand office, spreading out his morning reading material of an array of local newspapers in front of him, and then—according to the coroner's report—promptly went home to Jesus while leaving his earthly body dead in his chair.

Despite the fact Theo Sr. had been ninety-seven when he passed, it was a shock to know that he was mortal like everyone else. It was an even bigger shock when the shaggy, bearded grandson, who'd barely made a cameo at his grandfather's funeral, turned up in Savannah as the new Lucas on the office letterhead.

Julia had heard from scuttlebutt around the courthouse that Theo III had slipped right into his grandfather's position as senior partner at the firm despite the fact that he'd barely been out of law school long enough to qualify as a junior partner at any other firm in town. It hadn't taken an insider to know that the more senior attorneys, Kyler, Wilson, and Strong, were not pleased that a kid from Atlanta Legal Aid was occupying the office they had all aspired to. Such was the influence of Theo Sr. that, even from the grave, he was dictating who ran the law office in his absence.

At least the kid from Atlanta Legal Aid had seen the good sense in getting a haircut and having his beard groomed to a more socially acceptable length. Meredith predicted that in six months, when the summer heat hit Savannah, the beard would be gone altogether.

"My grandfather was fond of both of you," Theo said, interrupting her musings about his grooming. "Though he did profess a slight fear when he came before you on any sort of court matter," he added to Julia.

"I cannot imagine why," Julia said.

"According to him, you were the only judge who could see right through his blustering and tell him to get to the point."

"He did tend to be rather long-winded on occasion," Julia admitted with a wry smile. "But always entertaining. And he had a sharp legal mind."

"How can we help you?" Meredith asked, thinking she'd like this Theo to get to the point as well. At this rate, the funeral procession would leave without them and she and Julia would be forced to hike through Bonaventure Cemetery from the back of the parking lot in their heels.

"As I was saying, my grandfather held you both in high regard, so based on that recommendation of your character, I would like to talk to you about a case I am working on." He glanced around then back at them. "Not right here and now, of course. It wouldn't be appropriate, considering the circumstances. But perhaps later today? Or tomorrow?"

"My, you are in a hurry." Meredith exchanged a look with Julia. "Perhaps after the graveside service?" At her partner's nod, she returned her attention to Theo. "Do you know where we're located?"

"I do, and I'll be there after the graveside. Thank you, ladies."

Theo hurried off, leaving Meredith to watch him weave through the remaining stragglers on the sidewalk like a running back heading for the goal line. "Oh my, how he does hurry. What do you want to bet we get back from the graveside and find Theo waiting for us?"

"You think?" Julia said with a grin. "He seems anxious, so you might be right."

After making the hike Meredith had dreaded and listening to the pastor intone his words so softly that mosquitoes might have buzzed louder, she and Julia headed back toward their office. Meredith parked in her spot behind the building, and Julia used her key to open the back door and let them both in.

Cool air hit Meredith like a blessing from above, and she smiled. "Oh, that feels so good. Why in the world is it so warm and humid in November? Weren't we all wearing coats just last week?"

"Another cold front is coming, and we'll be back in our coats soon, or so Kate Collins, the weather lady on TV, says." Julia moved through the kitchen and headed toward the front of the building. "Meanwhile, we'll simply deal with the fact that it feels more like summer than fall today."

Meredith kicked off her shoes and reached into the fridge for a bottle of water. "I don't mind either. I would just like to know which season I'm going to get when I wake up in the morning."

"Kate would tell you, if you bothered to watch WSVG in the morning like I do," Julia called.

"The last thing I want to do in the morning is watch the news," Meredith responded as she followed her friend. "Although I do like Kate. And as long as we're stating facts, Kate wasn't on the show this morning, was she, smarty-pants?"

Julia laughed. "You've got me there. No, she wasn't. She was at the funeral."

Their assistant, Carmen Lopez, looked up from her desk and grinned. "Welcome back, ladies. There's a cute guy sitting on the steps. He hasn't buzzed to come in yet, though."

Julia walked to the door and looked out. "Carmen, go out and tell Theo we'll meet with him in the conference room, then grab waters for him and me, please."

"Theo? That's his name?" Her smile broadened. "I wonder if he's single. I've got a friend he'd be perfect for."

"Carmen," Julia said, her tone light as she shook her head. "He's here on business, but he cannot conduct that business out on the steps."

Carmen shrugged. "You two are no fun. I'll go get him, but he is cute and obviously employed, so I'm thinking they'd be perfect for each other."

"Please don't lead with that when you talk to him," Meredith said.

"Which part?" Carmen shrugged. "The 'my bosses are no fun' part or the 'you're a cutie and need to meet my friend' part?"

"How about the part where Carmen is looking for a new job?" Meredith asked with a grin.

Carmen giggled. "Oh please. I can't be gone five minutes without you calling to ask me where something is or how to do something."

Julia laughed. "Sad but true. Still, behave with Theo, okay?"

Carmen crossed her heart with her finger as if making a promise and then headed toward the door.

Meredith, still smiling at their assistant's antics, followed Julia down the hall. They could have hired someone more professional to work the front desk, but where would be the fun in that? Carmen was not only a great assistant, she also brightened the office with her youth and her effervescent personality, knew how to handle people, and was bilingual to boot.

Plus, she was right. Carmen did know where everything was. And when you worked for investigators who were busy handling other things, that job skill was priceless.

"You go on in," Julia said. "I'll be right there. I need to check something on my computer first."

Meredith nodded and stepped inside the conference room. Situated in the back of the first floor opposite Julia's office, for more than two decades the conference room had been her husband Ron's office. All of that changed when the remodel of the room was completed.

The walls had been repapered in a pale yellow silk that was true to the era of the home. Ron's old walnut desk had been moved to Meredith's office, and the rest of his office furniture was relegated to the attic at her house until the boys decided if they wanted any of it. In the center of the room, an elegant rosewood table, purchased at auction and rumored to once have been in the dining room at the governor's mansion, stood beneath a crystal chandelier.

Whether or not the story was true, Meredith loved the beautiful classic lines of the table and the six chairs that had come with the set. The armchairs, meant to go at the ends of the table, were now placed on either side of the fireplace and accessorized with tapestry pillows she'd found at a local antique store. The remaining four chairs were in pairs opposite each other at the table.

Lush Boston ferns on antique iron plant stands stood in front of each of the windows, softening the old shutters that had been repainted with the same warm ivory paint Meredith used on the woodwork in her office at home. Meredith had vetoed the plants as too much work, but Carmen had promised to tend the ferns, so they stayed.

While the room was lovely, a cozy haven and a sunny space where they could meet with clients, it was also the place that held the most memories of Ron. This was a good thing, she reminded herself as she let out a long breath. Good memories were the best way of remembering.

If only the good memories didn't still hurt just a little.

And on some days, maybe more than just a little.

Meredith settled at the table, facing the wall where Ron's plat map of historical Savannah now hung over the fireplace. Lots of good work had been done in this room. By her and by Ron.

"Thank You, Lord," she whispered, "that the work continues. May it be done to Your glory."

Chapter Two

"Are you all right, Meredith?"

She looked up to see Julia watching her from the door, a yellow legal pad in one hand and a silver pen in the other.

"Sure," she said. "Just still wondering if these ferns were a good idea." Not at all what she'd been thinking, and her friend had to know that.

Still, Julia nodded as she walked over to sit on the chair beside Meredith. "Given how Carmen dotes on the begonias, I think they'll do just fine in here."

"What do you think Theo Sr.'s grandson wants to talk about?" Meredith asked, hoping to avoid any further discussion about the conference room's décor or how she felt about it.

"I have no idea," Julia said. "He certainly seemed anxious to talk about it, whatever the topic."

A few minutes later, the door opened, and Theo Lucas III stepped inside. Carmen followed behind him to deliver the waters then stepped away to linger in the door, watching the young attorney as he positioned himself in a chair across from the ladies.

"Thank you, Carmen," Meredith said.

Carmen nodded and closed the door behind her. Theo immediately placed his briefcase on the table and opened it.

"Unlike my grandfather, I like to get right to the point." He pulled out two large envelopes and passed them across the table to Julia and Meredith. Then he retrieved a legal pad and a lovely gold and ebony Montblanc pen. "Have either of you heard of the Wilhelmina Styles Worthington will?"

Meredith gave Julia a sideways look then turned her attention to Theo. "Heard of it? You can't live in Savannah and not hear of that crazy old lady who left all her money, outside of what was tied directly to the family business, to her great-grandchildren."

"And you can't practice law in Georgia without hearing the arguments regarding the validity of that kind of exclusionary will in one form or another," Julia added. "I understand after many decades of legal wrangling, the will was finally declared valid four years ago."

"Coming up on five, I believe, but yes it was." He nodded to the envelopes. "You'll find a file-stamped copy of the will dated November 3, 1960, along with a few other documents and pleadings pertaining to the will challenge. There's also plenty of research material to look over, mostly in relation to the family tree. I took the liberty of making two copies of everything so you wouldn't have to share."

"Well, thank you." Meredith opened her envelope and retrieved the *Last Will and Testament of Wilhelmina Styles Worthington* from the top of the stack. Julia did the same.

"I'll save you the trouble of reading it all right now. My grandfather wrote the will and made sure it was done properly. Mrs. W. put everything in a trust that she could possibly put there. Money, stocks, property she had been gifted, all of it. And that trust has been sitting in the bank untouched since she died in 1977."

"That must be a nice nest egg," Julia said.

"I've ordered a forensic accounting of the trust to bring the amount up to current value, but considering the values of the stocks plus the way Savannah's property values have escalated in the intervening years, I think we're looking at something close to $100 million."

"You're joking," Meredith said on an exhale of breath.

"No wonder your grandfather's name was put at the front of the list of partners," Julia said. "Between managing that trust and fighting the will challenges, he must have made the firm a fortune."

"I wouldn't be able to comment on anything in regard to the firm, but I assure you I am quite serious about the value of the trust."

His expression told her that he was, but Meredith couldn't help but think of the young lawyer from his grandfather's funeral with his shaggy beard, long hair, and Led Zeppelin T-shirt who worked at a legal aid clinic in Atlanta. Stepping into your grandfather's senior partnership in a prestigious Savannah law firm sure could clean a fellow up in a hurry.

"Well then," Julia said politely, "I'm looking forward to reading these documents in detail later, but perhaps you can tell Meredith and me how we can help you."

"Now that the last Worthington grandchild has died, as we memorialized today, the trust must be distributed. That's where you ladies come in." Theo put away his pen and legal pad, closed his briefcase, and pressed his palms atop its worn black leather surface. "In an abundance of caution, our firm has decided to hire outside experts to determine who those heirs are."

"Us?" At Theo's nod, Julia continued. "Well, that is an interesting prospect. What can you offer as a starting point for the heir search?"

"That information is in the envelope as well. The forensic gene-alogist was able to put together a chart, but she wouldn't go so far as to say that there could be no other heirs. Nor, for that matter, would she say in complete certainty that Daniel Worthington did not have other children, although that much of the sordid tale does not come into play when determining the heirs."

"I don't understand," Meredith said. "As a former president of the historical society, I am very familiar with what a forensic gene-alogist does. Anyone worth their retainer ought to be able to certify that his or her work is complete. And if Daniel had more children..." She shrugged. "I guess it would make sense that Wilhelmina wouldn't recognize those as her heirs."

"Well, it is a $100 million risk she wouldn't take," he said slowly. "And this case is complicated."

"How so?" Julia asked.

"The will states that the heirs are the great-grandchildren. However, if you will notice in Article IV, section C, there is a clause that requires those great-grandchildren to be the issue of a legal marriage between their parents, one of whom is a grandchild of Mrs. W. through Simon or Thomas Worthington." He paused for effect. "Emphasis here being on the phrase 'legal marriage.'"

"Oh," Julia said. "So that excludes anyone who might have come to inheritance through a liaison with Daniel Worthington and a woman other than his wife. Except, of course, Simon Worthington, who was legally adopted by Daniel and Wilhelmina Worthington and thus considered as if he were born to them."

"That's right," he said. "The list of heirs must have either Simon or Thomas Worthington as a grandfather and be the product of a legal union between one of these men's offspring. Unofficially that list stands at three: Thomas Daniel Worthington III and the Worthington twins, Kenneth Worthington and Kate Worthington Collins. All three inherit through Thomas. We've not yet found anyone we can verify as a descendant of Simon."

"That's odd, don't you think?" Julia asked. "Someone as high profile as Simon Worthington not having anyone claiming to be his grandchild."

"From what I was able to glean from my grandfather, Simon was very different from his brother. He had an office in the building but wasn't much involved in the family business. Then he died—in 1961, I think—of the flu, leaving a wife and son. Simon's son, Ben, died in Vietnam in '69, then not long after, Simon's father, Daniel, died too. That would have been 1971. That left only Thomas to carry on the family business."

"Which he did," Meredith said. "The firm flourished."

"Yes, but there were rumors," Theo said, "that the son and his father, Thomas and Daniel, fought publicly at a board meeting the day before Daniel died. Some say his heart gave out due to the exertion. There was some confusion about his location when his heart gave out, which was thought to be proof someone was hiding something."

"Interesting," Meredith said.

"I asked Grandfather once if he thought Thomas played a part in his father's death. He dismissed that theory as balderdash."

"Theo Sr. did like that word. He used it often enough in my courtroom," Julia said with a chuckle. "As to Daniel's death, I recall from testimony given during the early days of the will's contest hearings that when called to the Worthington home to attend to the deceased, the coroner ended up with a black eye courtesy of someone at the scene."

"That is true," Theo said. "According to the records I recently read, the coroner later wrote a report stating that the body had been moved from the place of death to the room where he was found. The family took exception to that statement, preferring to stick with the story that their patriarch died peacefully in his bed. Neither the place of death nor the name of the person who hit the coroner was ever revealed."

"My granddaddy's money was on neither Thomas nor the help," Meredith said as Theo and Julia turned to look at her. "Granddaddy and his cronies would get together and start gossiping about days gone by in Savannah, and eventually one of them would bring up that story. He always said it was Mrs. Worthington who killed her husband, moved the body, then punched the coroner when he tried to assert his position over hers."

"You're joking," Theo said, his mouth gaping.

"Granddaddy never was. I'm just repeating what I overheard as I eavesdropped on those old men through the door as a kid." Meredith shrugged. "Apparently Mrs. W. ruled that house once her husband was destined for the family vault down at Bonaventure Cemetery, and the coroner was just the first one to find out." Meredith shifted positions and the direction of the conversation. "Back to our current dilemma. You've got a list of people who could be possible heirs, but we've got to qualify them by determining their parents were legally married to one another."

"At the time of their birth," Theo added. "And that's just part of the job. Since Mr. Thomas Worthington Jr.'s death aired on national news, our office has been inundated with calls and emails. Most of them are bogus and easily proven as such. However, not all of them can be so quickly dismissed. Once you've agreed to take on the assignment, I'll have the office courier deliver the paperwork on our prospectives."

"Prospectives?" Julia asked. "As in prospective heirs?"

"Yes," Theo said. "But be aware that these are completely unsolicited contacts. No one has gone through them, and there's no guarantee that any of them are even remotely related to the Worthingtons, much less that one of them is an heir."

"So we are clear," Meredith said, "what you need from us is a complete list of heirs who have been fully vetted as to their legitimacy. We do our own research but are also provided with your research as well as any correspondence from people who have contacted you and claimed a relationship to Mrs. Worthington."

"That sums it up," he told her. "Our office is willing to pay a retainer, half up front and the remainder at the time the trust is disbursed, since the costs will ultimately be borne by the estate. You'll find the details of the offer at the bottom of your stacks. If you'll just read the privacy statement carefully, sign, and initial it, we can get started."

"Not so fast," Meredith said. "Julia and I will need to discuss this and give you an answer once we've decided if we will take the case."

He shrugged. "I don't mind waiting outside if you'd like to talk now."

"No, you stay put. Julia?"

Julia nodded, snatched up her parcel of papers, and then followed as Meredith left the conference room and closed the door.

They moved back to the kitchen, and Meredith leaned against the counter.

"Well? What do you think?"

"Are you kidding me?" Julia said. "Who in their right minds would turn down a chance to work on this case? I would do it for free."

"As interesting as this case may turn out to be, we are not doing it for free," Meredith said.

Julia placed the stack of papers on the counter and scanned through them until she found the agreement. "Meredith," she said on a rush of breath, her eyes wide. "Look at what they want to pay us for this."

Meredith leaned in and spied the number that had her partner stunned. "That has to be a typo."

Julia shrugged. "My guess is we'll earn every penny of it before we're finished. There's a lot of responsibility that comes with determining who the heirs of $100 million are."

"But we're up to the task, don't you think?" Meredith asked.

Carmen came to stand in the doorway. "You two might want to take a look outside before you make any decisions on whatever that cutie in the conference room is asking you to do. It's about the Worthington will, right?"

"I would ask how you know that," Meredith said, "but I'll save you the time to explain. What's happening outside?"

"Just go look," she said. "And remember, you pay me to know what's going on."

Meredith hurried to the door and spied several news reporters out front standing on the sidewalk. "What in the world?"

"I asked that same question when that news guy with the comb-over came in with his camera crew from WSVG. He said he'd been tipped off that our office would be looking for the heirs of old Mrs. Worthington, and they wanted to get a statement from the two of you." She looked down at the floor then back at Meredith. "If it's true and you want to talk to them, I can let them in, but Meredith, you're going to need to put some shoes on."

Meredith laughed. "I cannot believe I have just conducted a meeting with the highest-paying potential client our firm has ever had and I was barefoot."

"Life is good," Julia said. "So should we go in and say we'll do it? And while we're at it, we'll also be telling him that if anyone speaks to the media and mentions us without a heads-up to us, we'll be charging double."

"Yes, of course!" Meredith said. "But let me find where I put my shoes first."

"There's one pair in the kitchen by the back door, two pair in your office under your desk, and another pair in the coat closet," Carmen said. "You wore the black pumps in the kitchen to the funeral, but I suggest you choose the silver flats under your desk. They look much better with your black dress. Trust me on this."

At Meredith's surprised look, Carmen laughed. "Like I said, you pay me to know what's going on."

Chapter Three

Wilhelmina Styles Worthington chose this precise moment to open the office door of Theophilus Tiberius Lucas Sr., and she found satisfaction in the surprise on his face as he looked up sharply. He hadn't expected her, which was exactly why she had chosen this moment to arrive.

She might turn sixty in a few weeks, but her timing was still as impeccable as her fashion sense. Better, perhaps.

A few minutes earlier, and Theo would likely not yet have become immersed in his newspaper reading and could have easily detected the sound of her red Chanel heels on the marble floors of the hall outside his door.

A few minutes later, and any number of attorneys or members of the prestigious Savannah law firm staff could have arrived and caught her letting herself in the locked back door of the building that used to house her daddy's bank.

In addition to tutoring her in the fine art of picking a lock, her father, George Washington Styles, had taught his only daughter two valuable lessons. First, always catch the other side unaware. And second, never miss the opportunity to keep your mouth shut.

She'd done both this morning, making quick use of the hairpin she'd stashed in her favorite Chanel handbag to open the back door as she'd done dozens of times when the building belonged to Daddy, and now, as she stood silently watching Theo try to figure out how she'd managed to show up here today.

For it wasn't just a locked door that had kept her out. There was also the troublesome issue of her involuntary confinement in a lovely but secluded institution that masqueraded as an elegant rest home for those whose genteel minds were temporarily or perhaps permanently troubled. Or, alternatively, for those whose families wished to conspire to quietly hide away an inconvenient relative.

The grandfather clock that had ticked for more than a century at some location or another in Savannah chimed the quarter hour. Still Wilhelmina kept her silence. She did, however, paste on a well-practiced smile as she closed the office door.

Let the traitor she'd thought was her friend wonder a little longer, she decided. Theo had plenty to answer for, thus the reason for her visit. She, however, owed him nothing.

So Wilhelmina stood very still in the doorway in the same Christian Dior dress and mink coat she'd walked out of confinement in, and waited. Let him wonder just a little longer.

"Willa," Theo said, showing his obvious surprise by referring to her with the name that only those closest to her used.

He folded his newspaper and set it aside, never breaking eye contact with her. Then, when she said nothing nor moved a muscle, the lawyer offered the beginnings of a grin.

The clock ticked relentlessly on, the even cadence filling the silence between them. Finally Theo shook his head. "I'm sorry, did we have an appointment that I forgot about?"

"We did not." Wilhelmina moved toward him as if she owned the place—since technically she had, until the last payment on the mortgage had been received thirteen years ago.

She settled herself on the chair across from his desk with her handbag at her side.

Theo sat back, an unreadable expression crossing his face. At three years shy of forty, the son of Greek immigrants had made his way up in the world swiftly and with good cause. Theo was not only a good attorney. He was the best lawyer in Savannah.

Wilhelmina had determined this years ago when she watched him blaze a trail through the complicated mess that Daddy had left behind when he died. Still wet behind the ears back then with a brand-new law degree and a bar card that hadn't been mailed out to him yet, Theo had been given a case that no one wanted.

Daddy hadn't been the most popular man in Savannah, even if he had been one of the wealthiest. He hadn't come by his money by being nice to people, a fact that made finding an advocate for the sole heir to his estate after his death all the more difficult.

Daniel had offered to step in and handle the situation, but even back then, when things were going along just fine and Daniel Worthington was still the love of her life, instinct had told her to keep her business and her husband's separate. So she declined all offers for assistance from her husband and went about a search for the right man for the job.

Had she put any credence in luck and coincidence— which she definitely did not—Wilhelmina would have believed she'd hit the jackpot with Theo. Instead, she'd known in her heart that God was looking out for her when He sent the young attorney to handle things.

Which made it all the more painful recently when it appeared that her own attorney had been part of Daniel and the boys' plot against her.

Theo was nervous. She watched him pick up the ivory and gold Montblanc pen she'd given him for Christmas last year and study it.

Finally he looked up to meet her steady gaze. "Then I'm going to have to ask you why you're here, Wilhelmina, because I don't have any idea."

"No," she said sweetly as she rested her gloved hands in her lap. "I don't suppose you do. But then I doubt you expected I would be out so soon."

"Out?" He shook his head. "I don't understand."

Wilhelmina frowned then quickly returned her expression to neutral. She hadn't considered the fact that Daniel and the boys wouldn't have let Theo in on their plan. He was, after all, the attorney who handled all of her business matters. And Daniel's personal legal work.

As she studied the lawyer closely, she decided he might be telling the truth. For the first time, she considered that he might not have known what Daniel and the boys were up to after all.

"Do you still represent Daniel on his personal matters?"

He shook his head. "Not for more than a year. I sent him elsewhere when I realized representing you both could be a conflict of interest."

She ought to ask for details, but knowing Theo, he wouldn't give them. He'd chosen her over Daniel, and that mattered.

"I suppose I should begin at the beginning, then," she said. "It all started several months ago. May, I believe it was. Or it might have been June. All I can say for certain is it was blasted hot in Savannah, and I thought a trip anywhere else that might offer a cool breeze sounded like a little slice of heaven."

"Daniel mentioned you'd gone away for a while." At her upraised eyebrows, he hastened to add, "I saw him on the golf course Labor Day weekend, I believe. Or maybe it was at a Chamber of Commerce meeting in October. I assumed you were at a spa or maybe touring Europe with friends."

She waved away the comment. "He was right. I did go away, but I don't suppose he offered any details."

"He did not."

"No, he wouldn't have." Wilhelmina paused to consider her words carefully. "My husband and sons conspired together to have me put away, Theo. What I thought was a lovely vacation on the beaches of Hawaii for a few weeks turned out to be a one-way trip to a padded cell."

Theo's gasp filled the space between them and answered the question of whether he was in on the plans with absolute certainty. He definitely was not.

"But why?" he asked. "There's absolutely nothing wrong with you, Willa."

Again, the endearment. She smiled, and this time it was genuine.

"Nervous exhaustion, or some such nonsense, was what Daniel claimed. He said I was a danger to myself and others." Wilhelmina paused. "And in a way, I was, I suppose. His board of directors wouldn't have liked to hear the tales I could have told them about what my husband was up to when he thought his wife wasn't looking. And my sons, I'm sorry to say, aren't much better."

The boys—her sons—were a heartache that plagued her much worse than anything her husband had done. Though she had not given birth to Simon, she'd loved him equally to Thomas and raised him no different than his brother.

Simon had come to the family quietly back in 1927, as things were done back then. The explanation was a young woman from the secretarial pool at Daniel's company had found herself in a difficult situation just when it appeared the Worthingtons might lose their only son to the health issues that had plagued him since birth.

The timing was perfect, Daniel had argued. A blessed coincidence. God was providing a second child for them in case He decided to take their firstborn.

It had seemed so good. So right.

Only Wilhelmina did not believe in coincidences. And Daniel had forgotten to mention that he was Simon's biological father. That knowledge had come on the day she'd stumbled upon a birth certificate in a vault at the bank while looking for her grandmother's pearl brooch to wear on Easter Sunday.

If only she'd listened to Daddy and kept her mouth shut about what she'd learned. Instead, Wilhelmina had gone after Daniel with guns blazing. Figuratively, of course, not literally. Shooting a husband simply wasn't done in their social circle, even if the situation warranted it.

"I am such a fool, Theo," she murmured, pushing away the thoughts with a wave of her gloved hand. "But not so much of a fool that I wasn't able to get myself out of the trap they'd laid for me. I managed it because my daddy raised me to handle my business when I needed to, as you know. I did what I had to do to make the doctors listen to reason, and now here I am."

Even as she said the words, Wilhelmina wondered if the amount she'd paid the team of high-priced psychologists and physicians was more than what it cost for Daniel to put her away in the first place. Not that it mattered. She'd done what it took to remove herself from a place where she didn't belong.

Not for the first time, and probably not for the last time either.

"Here you are indeed," Theo said, surprise still lacing his voice. "What can I do for you?"

"I want to write a new will," she said firmly, her eyes never wavering from her attorney's face. "Everything that's mine—and I mean every single thing I own from what Daddy left me to what Daniel has used my name to purchase—is to go into a trust."

"All right." He retrieved a legal pad from his desk drawer and placed it in front of him. "Have you decided who all of the beneficiaries of the trust will be? I'll need the names to complete the documents."

She smiled. "That's where this gets tricky. I don't know their names, because they haven't been born yet."

Theo set the pen down and frowned. "Explain, please."

Wilhelmina squared her shoulders and prepared for the battle to come. Theo wouldn't like what she had to say, but he would do as she asked, and he would do it in a way that no one could undo. It was why she paid him so well.

"I wish to leave the entirety of my estate to my great-grandchildren, and I do not want a penny to be paid out until the last of my grandchildren is dead and buried."

"Willa," Theo said softly, "think carefully about what you'd be doing if you go through with this. You'd be telling not just Thomas and Simon but their children too, that you want none of your estate to go to them. In my experience, the person who has been left out takes that as a lack of love."

She waved away the statement with a sweep of her hand. "Oh, that's ridiculous. I love Simon and Thomas with all my heart, and they know it. I'm sure. However, those boys fell in with their father in this scheme to send me away and take over my business interests."

"But the grandchildren too, Willa?"

Theo sat very still. He was waiting for her to say more. To explain herself. Thus, she continued.

"Daniel was set to vote my shares at the next board meeting of the bank, where he would be changing the charter and putting himself in control of the whole shebang with Simon and Thomas as his vice presidents. My grandfather started that bank, and my daddy built it into what it is today. Of all the nerve." Wilhelmina paused to collect herself. "Did you know about that, Theo? Because if you did know, I'll find out. I always do. Better to admit to it now."

"I did not," he said crisply. "And for the record, I had no idea you were being railroaded into a rest home by your family."

"I was institutionalized, Theo, but I assure you it was for reasons that had nothing to do with my mental health or any sort of need for rest."

He nodded. "Then no offense to you, Willa, but I'll need a doctor's certification that you are of sound mind. If I don't have that, then you know what will happen. One or both of *your boys—or Daniel if he were to survive you—will challenge the will on the grounds that you were unfit when the document was drafted. If not one of them, then one of your grandchildren. It'll be an easy case to prove considering what you've just told me. They'll win then, and you'll be left with the last will you signed, which gives Daniel everything with the boys as equal beneficiaries* per stirpes. *I can guarantee it."*

The truth. But she had anticipated as much.

She opened her handbag and retrieved the envelope she'd brought for this purpose. She slid it across the desk toward Theo. "Do your due diligence and make all the phone calls you need to make. Along with the doctor's letter, I've taken the precaution of writing a letter of permission to allow you to talk about my medical history with my physicians."

"You've thought of everything." He tucked the envelope into his desk drawer without opening it. "However, I would be remiss in my duties if I didn't try to talk you out of this. You love your boys. You'll forgive them, even if you don't find it in your heart to forgive your husband. What if you die before you fix a will that no longer represents how you feel about them?"

"I do love my boys. But I won't change my mind about this. This isn't about how I feel about Thomas and Simon. They allowed money to sway them. Daniel added substantial amounts to their trust funds the same day that their affidavits agreeing to their father's claims about me were signed. What does that tell you?"

"It tells me I'm glad my son is still young enough that I don't have to worry about his loyalty to me. But I do see

what you're saying. However, why not give it to the grandchildren?"

"Thomas Jr., Spencer, and Ben can benefit from the money already in trust funds set up by their grandfather. Likely my husband has cut me out of anything I might have coming to me in that trust—not that I want it, thank you very much. Daddy set me up just fine, and I've got a good head for business. But my grandchildren? They will not go hungry, nor will their parents. What I have will go to the blood relatives I leave behind in the generation after them who are not here to witness all this greed." Her temper flared. "Why all the questions?"

"These are the questions I will be asked when the will challenges begin to come in. And that is if I choose to write this will at all, which I have not yet decided to do." He gave her a pointed look. "As I've already said, you can rest assured this document, should it be written as you've requested, will be tangled up in court challenges for years. Decades, perhaps. It'll be a nightmare."

Wilhelmina shrugged. "Think of that as job security for you, Theo. And be sure to write into the will that you'll be handling any challenge that comes along. Give yourself a partnership in this firm, if it can be arranged. I would hate for you not to benefit from the circus that is surely to follow my demise. I wish you a nice long life and a good income from that defense."

"Willa," he said gently, "the last thing I want to do is benefit from your demise."

"Which is exactly why you shall. Unlike any of my family members who are alive right now." She retrieved a second envelope and set it on the desk in front of her. After a moment's hesitation, Wilhelmina pressed it toward Theo then sat back in the chair.

On the street outside, a horn honked. Here in Theo's office, the grandfather clock continued an even cadence.

Theo picked up the envelope. "What is this?"

"Open it," she said.

He did as she asked. "I cannot take this," he said after pulling out the check that she'd placed inside. "I know you claim you're sane, but do you realize this is a check for one million dollars?"

"I am acutely aware of the exact amount, Theo. I came here this morning with the intention of throwing that check in your face and telling you that was the retainer you'd lost out on because you'd taken sides with my husband and sons in having me shipped off."

"And now?" he asked.

"And now I know you had no part in all of that nonsense, so I would like to place you on retainer for legal services in regard to my last will and testament with that check serving as the first deposit."

"A million dollar retainer for writing a will? I don't know what to say."

She paused. "I need you, Theo. The will is just the first thing that has to be done. There will be other battles to be fought. If he outlives me, Daniel will be relentless. He will stop *at nothing to see that our sons remain loyal to him. You'll earn that first million and probably a few million more before it's all said and done, so put a clause in my will that covers your fees for defending the new will. I'm just sorry that, when the time comes, I won't be here to see how you manage it."*

"Forgive me, but that all sounds very dramatic." He let the envelope drop to the desk. "Are you sure you're not over-stating the problem?"

"I was put into a mental institution by my husband with the blessing and assistance of my sons. Does that sound dra-matic to you?"

"It does, actually," Theo said. "But I will investigate all of this, and if what you've said is true, only then will I accept the retainer and the job of defending you that goes along with it."

"You will find that it is," she said.

Theo only smiled in response.

She let out a long breath and then stood. "You let me know when you've made up your mind. Just one thing: what we've said here today is to remain between us. I haven't yet let Daniel or the boys know I'm home from my little vacation. I'd hate it if my surprise was ruined."

"Of course," he assured her. "You have my word. How can I find you?"

Wilhelmina gave the question some thought. She ought to trust him enough to let him know she'd be staying at Daddy's fishing cottage out on the island. It was safe, secluded, and had never been on the books, so no one would think to look for her there.

Still, she wasn't quite ready to put all her cards on the table. Not until after her will was written and put away in the vault at Theo's office for safekeeping.

"I'll find you," she finally told him. "Will three days be enough time?"

"I'll see that it is," Theo said.

"Fine. Then I'll be back here Friday morning." She paused again. "Same time."

"I'll leave the back door unlocked," he told her.

Wilhelmina's smile was swift and broad as she stood. "No need."

"Because you have a key?" he asked with a half grin.

She merely smiled and then left him wondering about the answer to that question as she retraced her steps to the door. Daddy would have been proud.

Chapter Four

THE NEXT AFTERNOON, MEREDITH LOOKED up from the papers spread across her desk to find Julia watching her from the doorway, her purse slung over her shoulder. "Going somewhere?"

"I've got some errands to run downtown, and I need a walk. Want to come with me or need anything?"

She shrugged. "Maybe a coffee if you're picking up anything to bring back here."

"Sure," Julia said as her eyes slid across Meredith's desk. "How long have you been at that?"

Meredith leaned back and stretched her back then did the same with her arms. Her neck was tight, but there was no good fix for that. Not until she got home tonight and took a hot shower.

"The better part of an hour, but I really need to keep at it."

The scope of the task ahead of them was finally becoming clear to her. She sighed. It was a massive job. The course of their investigation was fraught with possibilities for getting it wrong.

Then there was the ongoing issue of dealing with the news media. They'd sent Carmen out to let the reporters know there would be no statement from their firm.

Meredith was no fool, however. That tactic might have worked today, but as persuasive as their assistant had been, it was a temporary fix to what could become a permanent press problem.

A problem they would eventually need to address. Along with so many more.

She leaned back in her chair and looked up at Julia as she sighed. "We were right in taking this case, weren't we?"

"Of course we were." Julia settled onto the chair across the desk and shrugged. "How could we not? This isn't just any case. It's one with historical significance. And it's fascinating, don't you think?"

"*Fascinating* is one of the words I've used in the past hour. *Frustrating, confusing,* and *downright befuddling* also come to mind." Meredith shook her head. "How does one family come to all of this? Such a wealth of money and a poverty of feelings. Or at least that's how it seems to me."

"Don't be so sure that the decedent didn't do this out of love," Julia said. "Without knowing the full story, we can't say. But maybe that was her intention."

"To cut her children and grandchildren out of her will is an act of love?" Meredith shook her head. "I don't see it."

"Well, neither do I," Julia said, "but I'm just saying that we can't know what Mrs. Worthington's thoughts were when she drafted this document. The one thing that isn't in our packet, or so it seems, given the size of it, are the attorney's notes. That might have allowed us to step into the mind of the testatrix. But since those notes are absent, we'll never know if she told her attorney why she was doing this."

"Whatever the reason, the results are just sad, Julia," Meredith said.

"I agree. I didn't preside over a lot of probate matters during my judicial career, but the cases that found their way into my court were almost always tragic. It's just so sad what money—or the lack of it—can do to a person."

"As long as I knew Tommy Two and his family, I never thought to ask him what it was like growing up as a Worthington. I can't imagine it would have been easy."

"He seemed to make the best of it," Julia offered. "He was a kind and generous man, and he did fine without the inheritance that skipped his generation and the one before. Maybe it was a blessing that he had to work for what he got."

"To be fair, Mrs. Worthington only put into trust what belonged to her," Meredith reminded her. "Tommy Two still had sizable holdings. I doubt it took much work to maintain that bank balance."

"I wonder who will get those, now that Tommy Two's only child has disappeared." Julia paused. "You know we have to find Trey, right? Or at least find out if he's alive."

"Good point." Meredith glanced down at the papers littering her desk and then back up at her partner. "We've got to track down heirs who qualify and, if they're not living, then we qualify *their* heirs, so I propose we start a list. Maybe a family tree that we can fill in with marriages—"

"Very important we prove those are valid," Julia interjected.

"Yes, absolutely. A paper trail is going to be essential. We'll have to find birth and marriage records for anyone who goes onto the chart."

"Certified copies," Julia added. "I don't want to take any chances on ending up with a forged or altered copy of a birth certificate or marriage license. If someone goes on the list, it is because we've gone above and beyond to prove they belong there."

"Agreed," Meredith said and then sighed again. "One hundred million dollars split among the people on a list we create."

"And certify that it's complete. Let's not forget that," Julia said. "We don't want to leave off anyone who should be mentioned. Imagine the lawsuit we could face if we miss someone."

"Yes. And no, thank you. I do not want to imagine that."

Silence fell between them as Meredith considered the gravity of their situation. Finally, she shrugged. "If anyone is up to the task of finding the Worthington heirs it's us, so enough of that. Let's get to work."

"I'll be right back." Julia hurried out only to return a moment later with a legal pad and her favorite silver pen, her errands obviously postponed. "I propose we start with a list of what we know. I'll take notes."

Meredith grinned. "All right, well, we know for certain that Tommy Two's son, Trey, is an heir. Where is he? Is he even alive? That's anyone's guess. But that's a problem we'll face once our list is complete. Tommy's widowed sister-in-law, Sunny, has the twins, which makes a total of three known heirs. Who else?"

"That's the big question. Are there more?" Julia shrugged. "I think we're going to have to start at the beginning and work forward from Mrs. Worthington's children on down and develop our own family tree."

"We can start with this." Meredith sifted through the papers until she found what she was looking for then slid the stapled stack of pages toward Julia. "Our forensic genealogist's work."

"Work that she won't certify as complete," Julia added. "I suppose she's concerned with liability."

"We should be as well. We have to be absolutely certain that the names we put on our list are verified and authentic." Meredith paused. "I think it's safe to start with Trey Worthington. Tommy Two's wedding to Katherine made the *New York Times* back in the midseventies. We can confirm with a records search, but I don't think we'll have a problem verifying him."

"No," Julia countered. "The problem comes in actually finding Trey to make sure he's still alive. I'll poke around in the records of the trial and see what I can find out. Failing that, I'll make some calls. With any luck I'll come up with a paper trail that leads us to heir number one."

"Is that what we're calling him now?" Meredith asked with a chuckle.

Carmen appeared in the doorway with a worried look. "I've got a delivery here for the two of you from Lucas, Wilson, Kyler & Strong."

"Yes, we're expecting it. Just have the courier bring the documents in here," Meredith told her.

"In your office?" Carmen tilted her head. "Are you sure?"

"Yes, is there something wrong?"

"You should probably come and see this." She stepped into the hall and gestured toward the corridor then moved out of the way. "Both of you."

Meredith expected to see a law office courier carrying a file of papers, or perhaps a small box of them. Instead, she found a scowling delivery driver waiting for her. Propped against the wall was a hand cart filled to the top with a stack of boxes.

"I'm sorry, ladies," Carmen said. "I tried to handle this, but he wouldn't cooperate. Apparently it doesn't matter that I am the one who signs for deliveries in this office."

"Which one are you?" the driver called when he spied Meredith. "I'm supposed to see that only a Meredith or a Julia takes delivery." He cast a sideways look at Carmen. "I'm sorry, but she couldn't show identification that she was either, so I can't let her sign."

"I'm Meredith," she told him. "And considering how many boxes there are, I think the conference room is probably the right place to put them for now."

"Fine," he told her, "but I need an ID first."

Julia pressed past her to retrieve her identification from her wallet. "This should work," she said as she presented it to the courier. "And I agree. Put those in the conference room, please. Ms. Bellefontaine will show you her ID and sign for delivery when you're done." She looked back over her shoulder at Carmen. "I'm bringing coffee from the Bean for Meredith once I finish my errands downtown. Do you want your usual?"

"Double shot, extra whip," Carmen said with a grin. "Dash of cinnamon and cayenne. A little sweet and a little spicy, just like me."

"Coming right up. Well, in a half hour or so," Julia called as she stepped around the courier and disappeared out the front door.

"What is all of this?" Carmen's attention followed the courier as he pushed the handcart down the hallway toward the conference room.

"I believe those are the contact forms Theo told us about." At Carmen's confused look, Meredith continued. "Apparently there was a news report about the Worthington will, and ever since, the firm has been getting emails and calls from potential heirs."

Carmen's perfectly arched brows rose. "And you're planning to read all of them?"

"We have to," Meredith said as she made the trip across her office to retrieve her wallet containing her ID from her desk. "What if there's a legitimate heir in all of that and we miss him or her by not doing our due diligence?"

The phone rang at Carmen's desk, and she frowned. "Good luck with that. I've got to catch this."

"Sign here," the courier said as he reappeared from the conference room with an empty cart.

Meredith presented her ID, accepted the clipboard from his outstretched hand, and hastily scribbled her name in the spot he indicated. She accepted the yellow receipt that had been torn from the clipboard and returned her wallet to her desk before heading toward the conference room. She had no idea where to begin to sort the data she'd just received.

"Meredith," Carmen called, "you might want to take this call. It's a lady about the Worthington will. I've got her on hold."

"And so it begins," she said under her breath. Louder, she called, "Take a message, please."

Carmen came to the door. "Are you sure? She sounds like she knows what she's talking about."

Meredith gave the statement a moment's thought. "That may be true, but right now I'm a little overwhelmed with the scope of this project. Please get a detailed message including contact information and thank her for calling."

Carmen didn't bother to hide her disappointment. "I really think she's got some helpful information on Simon Worthington's side of the family. She's naming names and quoting dates so fast I can't write them all down."

"She might know something that will help us or she might not," Meredith said. "But right now I'm just not able to give her the attention she needs. Please, just talk to her. It would be very helpful to me right now if you did that. Just get all the details, and I'll handle the rest."

Carmen hurried back to her desk. "Tell me everything," Meredith heard her say. "And don't leave out a single detail. I'll stop you if I have questions. But please slow down. I can't write as fast as you're talking."

Meredith stepped into the conference room to confront the four boxes that were neatly stacked in the corner. Taped to the topmost box was a large brown envelope.

By the time Julia returned with her coffee, Meredith had filed the receipt for the boxes and was poring over the contents list she'd found in the envelope. She gratefully accepted the cup and smiled. "Your timing is perfect," Meredith told her. "I just unlocked the key to the kingdom." She took a sip of the delicious brew then grinned at Julia's confused look. "Okay, so I made that up, but I did figure out a shortcut to analyzing all of this data."

"I hope so." Julia tossed her purse onto a chair and settled at the conference table with her coffee in hand. "I was trying to think of how we would be managing that much information. I'm glad you've got a plan."

Meredith pointed to the flash drive in her laptop's USB port. "Theo sent us a spreadsheet that lists everything that's in the boxes. I can sort by date or name or any number of ways."

"Oh, tell me more," Julia said. "Have you already tried it?"

"I decided to go back to see how long ago these emails and calls started coming in, so I sorted the data by date and went forward from there." She paused. "I found something interesting. One woman has been calling and emailing the firm for more than ten years. And get this. Her name is Willadeane Worthington. She claims to be named after her great-grandmother."

"Interesting." Julia took a sip of coffee and looked over at the stack of boxes before returning her attention to Meredith. "Is she the only one who's been a persistent contact?"

"So far," Meredith said. "Everyone else has either called or emailed no more than a few times, and most did it right after the news feature ran. I'm just scanning what's there, though, so don't hold me to that, but I think it's probably wise to start at the beginning with these contact forms. Start with the oldest ones first."

"I agree. We have a big job ahead of us," Julia said. "I'm not up for tackling anything else this afternoon, but I propose we meet tomorrow to decide how we're going to divide up the tasks that need to be done."

"Agreed," Meredith said as she closed her laptop. "These names and dates are starting to run together."

Carmen tapped on the door then stuck her head inside. "Wow," she said. "That was some conversation."

"Are you just now hanging up with her?" Meredith checked her watch. "You've been on the phone almost twenty minutes."

"I know, but she had some good stuff. I really think you need to talk to this lady, Meredith." Carmen handed her two pages of notes written on a legal pad. "She's been trying to get someone to listen to her story for more than ten years but can't get anyone to pay attention."

"Ten years?" Julia asked. "What's her name?"

Meredith looked down at the note and then up at Julia. "Her name is Willadeane Worthington."

"The same woman who's been contacting Lucas, Wilson, Kyler & Strong all these years," Julia said. "I wonder what her story is. She's certainly persistent."

"There's only one way to find out," Carmen told them. "Which of you plans to call her?"

Meredith stood and shook her head. "Not me. We've done enough work on this case today. I'm taking my coffee and going home. What about you, Julia?"

Julia rose, coffee in hand, and retrieved her purse. "I agree with Meredith. It's been a long and eventful day. Let's start fresh tomorrow."

"Does that mean me too?" Carmen asked. "Because it's not five o'clock yet."

"It's five o'clock somewhere," Meredith told her. "Go on home. We'll lock up. But first, please call Willadeane Worthington and make an appointment for a conference call with both of us. Check our calendars to be sure we're both free."

"No, I like setting them when you're busy," Carmen said in a teasing tone as she disappeared into the hallway. Then she popped back in. "Just so we're clear, I'm going to be paid as if I stayed until five, right?"

"Yes," Meredith said.

"Good, and thank you. You're not the only one who likes cute shoes, Meredith. I've got my eyes on the cutest red leather boots, but I can't afford them if I'm going to be docked for leaving early."

Julia and Meredith exchanged looks and laughed.

"Remember those days?" Julia asked. "When buying new boots took precedence over paying for chiropractors and mortgages."

"Barely," Meredith told her. "Now I'm really tired. Let's go home."

Julia frowned. "I'll have to call Beau. He was going to pick me up at five."

"Call him and tell him I'll drop you off." Meredith smiled. "Want to take a box home with you to review?"

Julia groaned. "Sure, why not? I assume you'll be doing the same thing."

"Unfortunately, yes." Meredith paused. "But it beats spending the evening following a cheating spouse for a client or trying to catch an insurance fraudster cleaning out his gutters when he's supposed to be immobile in a cast."

"True," Julia said. "And this pays better."

"Much better," Meredith agreed. "I just hope it's worth what we have to do to get that ridiculously large paycheck."

Chapter Five

THE UNSEASONABLY WARM TEMPERATURES FROM earlier in the week had blown out with the strong cold front that crashed through Savannah yesterday afternoon like a poorly behaved relative at the buffet line. Meredith had already fended off questions from Chase this morning regarding Thanksgiving plans.

What was it about cold weather in November that made her youngest son start thinking about what to serve on Turkey Day? But then, he'd always loved the holiday ever since he was a little boy.

Meredith sighed and turned her attention to the fire crackling in the fireplace. If there was a more lovely office in Savannah, she didn't know of it. The renovation of the old building last spring had been a wise decision. If only Ron had lived to see what they'd done with the place where he'd toiled all those years.

She glanced over at the corner of her desk and the silver frames filled with smiling faces of the children and grandchildren Ron wouldn't see around the table at Thanksgiving again this year. It was two years in September since they lost him, but thinking of that empty chair at the head of the table still broke her heart.

Her phone dinged with a text, and Meredith reached for it. QUIN CROWLEY.

Immediately she thought of her good friend's quick smile and the way he made her laugh as she tapped on the screen. Busy this evening? he'd asked.

A knock at the door jolted her. Carmen stood in the doorway. "That Worthington lady is here. I put her in the conference room and am getting her a cup of coffee."

"Thank you," Meredith said. "Is Julia back from the post office?"

"Not yet, but she texted a few minutes ago to say the lines were long and she might be late, so you should start without her."

"All right. Would you mind grabbing me a cup of coffee too? Tell Ms. Worthington I'll be right in."

"Will do, boss," Carmen said.

Meredith gathered up the file she'd been given by Theo on the possible Worthington heir and stood. She got halfway to the door when she thought better of ignoring that text.

Once she returned to her desk, she set the file down and shot off a quick response.

What do you have in mind?

Then she pressed Send before she could talk herself out of it and hurried out the door, file in hand. Carmen met her at the conference room door with two cups of coffee.

"Thank you," Meredith said as she offered her a smile then followed her inside.

Willadeane Worthington insisted on meeting Julia and Meredith in person rather than settling for a phone call. Thus, the petite blond woman in dark jeans, crisp white shirt, and a tailored navy blazer was seated in the conference room with a smile on her perfectly made-up face and a thick file of papers encased in a pink floral port-folio in front of her.

If Meredith had to base her opinion of Willadeane's sanity on appearances alone, she would believe everything the woman said. From her perfectly styled shoulder-length hair to the way she made intelligent small talk with Carmen about how best to keep a sour-dough starter alive while they waited for Julia to join them, this lady did not seem like a crackpot.

And yet, according to the file Meredith had read, this Willadeane had legally changed her last name to the same name as the decedent. And spent ten years attempting to get into a will. If she wasn't legit, she was either not entirely sane or a very determined crook.

"Thank you for coming in," Julia said as she stepped into the conference room, interrupting Meredith's thoughts. "I'm sorry I was late. The post office lines were long today."

"Actually, we were just getting started." Meredith smiled and turned her attention to their guest. "Ms. Worthington, I'm sure you know why we've asked you to come in."

She tapped the file in front of her. "Please call me Willadeane. And of course I do. You've finally read my letters, emails, and phone messages. Your assistant told me that on the phone when she called to make the appointment."

"Not all of them, I'm afraid, though we will get to them all as soon as we can," Julia told her. "But we did see on the message log that you were the first one to contact Lucas, Wilson, Kyler & Strong in regard to Mrs. Worthington's will."

"And you're the one who has contacted them the most," Meredith added.

"I'm persistent," Willadeane said. "But for good reason. I am who I say I am, and I've got plenty of proof. I'm sure you're hearing that from a lot of others who want to cash in now that Mr. Worthington has died, but I'm not one of them."

"No?" Meredith gave her a pointed look. "But you must realize that we have to check your story very carefully because the trust is quite lucrative?"

At Theo's request, the decision had been made not to discuss the details of the trust—especially the amount—with any of the prospective beneficiaries or the press. The mention of $100 million did tend to be distracting. Better to discuss the person and not what they might possibly receive.

"Of course I realize that," she said. "You can ask me anything. When I first learned who I was—that my grandfather was Simon Worthington—I thought, you know, it took a long time for me to find this out. I'm not going to sit back and be quiet about it."

"So that's why you've kept contacting the law firm over the years?" Julia asked her.

"I was just trying to find out about my kin. Back then, we didn't have as much online to search through as we do now, so it was quite the task to put together my family tree. I did it, though, and here I am."

"Here you are," Meredith echoed.

"I think we've gotten a little ahead of things," Julia said. She checked the file in her hands. "You weren't born Willadeane Worthington."

A statement, not a question. Still, Meredith was curious how she would explain herself.

"No ma'am," she said with no obvious signs of discomfort. "I took that name later on when I realized it fit me better. I'm sure you've already looked that up and found out I changed my name here in this county seven years ago."

"We'd rather you tell us about all of it," Julia said. "Start at the beginning from the moment you determined you were a Worthington heir and then walk us through the name change and how you ended up here in our office."

"There's a lot to that," Willadeane said.

"We've got time," Meredith assured her.

"And a strong interest in getting to the truth," Julia added.

Willadeane nodded. "My mama didn't tell me the story of who I was until it was almost too late. I don't know when she knew it, for that matter. She claims Daddy did all the wheeling and dealing that brought me home while she just prayed for a baby, then loved on the one she got. It was how things were done then."

Meredith took notice of those last words. Hadn't she just heard them recently in her meeting with Theo? If Willadeane and Theo were to be believed, quietly acquiring children—or passing them on to someone else—was done far too frequently in the Worthington family.

Willadeane's voice cracked, and tears welled up in her eyes. Julia reached for a tissue and handed it across the table to her.

"Thank you," she said as she dabbed at her eyes. "It's a hard story to tell in places. I still miss my mama, but I promised myself when she was on her deathbed that I wouldn't let this go. The Worthingtons didn't want me, but now they're stuck with me."

She set the tissue aside and opened her file. After retrieving two packets of paper held together by a rose-gold clamp at the top of each, she gave one to Julia and the other to Meredith.

"What is all this?" Meredith asked her.

"Some of the paperwork I've collected over the years while I was searching for my family. I've got lots more than this, but I figured this would get you started."

Julia pressed her hands atop the stack. "We'll look this over carefully, but first just tell us about yourself, Willadeane. As Meredith said, start at the beginning. I want to hear it in your own words."

Willadeane smiled. "First and foremost, thank you for listening. Nobody else has done that. I promise I won't waste your time."

"I'm glad to hear it," Meredith said. "When did you first claim you were a beneficiary of Mrs. Worthington's will?"

Willadeane gave Meredith the oddest look. It began as a blank stare and then slowly grew into the beginnings of a scowl.

"Have we offended you?" Julia asked.

"You might have if I let you," Willadeane said, "but I understand why you've got to ask such a thing in that way, though you've already sort of asked that already. I'm sure you're hearing from lots of people who want their cut of the money."

"And you don't?" Meredith asked.

"There's no good answer here," she said. "So I'll give you the true one. What I wanted when I first tried to get the attention of the Worthingtons had nothing to do with money." She shifted her attention from Meredith to Julia. "I just wanted a family." She shook her head. "Until I found out I was Daniel's great-granddaughter through his son Simon, I had no knowledge of my biological family. I was adopted, and while my adopted parents were the best in every way, I was still curious who I was before I was theirs." She paused and snatched up the tissue again. "I didn't do anything about it while my mama was alive. Toward the end, I was her caretaker. Daddy's too. It would have broken their hearts to know I was looking for my birth family."

"What changed your mind?" Meredith asked her.

"Once they both passed, I thought it was time to start my search at places like the adoption agency that handled my adoption and the hospital where I was born."

"How did you know those things?" Julia asked. "Most adoption cases I handled as a judge included a provision that this information was sealed, especially the older cases. The exception to this would be open adoptions, which this decidedly would not have been if what you are saying is true."

"It's true. Mine was sealed too, so it definitely was not any sort of open adoption. If it had been, I wouldn't have had to work so hard to find my family."

Willadeane paused to worry with the tissue in her hand. Meredith watched several expressions cross her face, but no more tears emerged. Finally she let out a long breath and nodded as if signaling that she was ready to speak again.

Willadeane met Meredith's steady gaze. "I knew the names of the adoption agency and the hospital where I was born from the paperwork I found hidden in my daddy's desk drawer. It was in a plain white envelope hidden under the organizer where he kept his pens and paper clips. If I close my eyes, I can still see it."

Meredith had memories like that, images that came when her eyes were closed. If this woman was lying, she was good at it.

A wry smile rose as Willadeane continued. "He caught me snooping when I was eleven. I only saw that much before he snatched it up and sent me out of his office. It was the only time I can ever remember my daddy yelling at me. My mama? Oh, absolutely, but never Daddy except that once. Next time I went to look, it was gone. I never found it again after that."

"How did you know to look there?" Meredith asked.

Willadeane chuckled. "I didn't know a thing about where to look, because I wasn't looking for anything in particular. I was a just nosy kid who saw an opportunity to snoop and took it. If I remember right, it was summertime and my parents were hosting a barbeque. Everyone was outside, and I was curious. Daddy's office was off-limits. I had free run of the house, but that door remained closed, and I was not supposed to go inside. So, of course, I had to see what the big deal was."

"And you found out the big deal was that you were adopted?" Meredith asked.

"Oh no." She waved away the question with a swipe of her hand. "My parents were very open about that. I'd known since I was a little girl. The curiosity about who I used to be before I belonged to them didn't blossom until later. Finding that document in Daddy's desk set a fire in me to answer that question."

"So after your parents passed, you decided to get your answer," Julia supplied.

"Yes. By the time I took a DNA test, I already knew who I was and had changed my name."

"Why change your name, though?" Meredith asked.

"This is not going to be easy to explain." She paused, looking up at the ceiling before continuing, once again worrying the tissue as she spoke. "I was my mama and daddy's daughter as long as they were alive on this earth, and in my heart they will always be my parents. But I found myself wondering if I had other relatives out there. Birth parents, aunts, uncles, grandparents, or even half siblings. I started looking at people on the street to see if they looked like me."

"That had to be difficult," Julia said, "but in my years as a judge, when someone came into my courtroom asking me to legally change their name, they always stated a reason. What specifically was yours?"

"Was it to attract the attention of the Worthington family?" Meredith supplied, watching the woman's face carefully as she spoke the words.

"In part, of course," Willadeane said. "Hearing you're related to someone with the same name as you tends to make more sense."

Meredith failed to see the logic in this statement but kept her opinion to herself. Instead, she kept her silence and waited for Willadeane to continue.

"The main reason, though, was because the name just plain fit. I was Amy Calloway before I knew who my people were. And that name fit me just fine. Then my mama and daddy went to be with Jesus and here I was, Amy Calloway on paper but a Worthington by birth. I settled on Willadeane as a tribute to both my mamas."

"That's nice," Julia said.

Willadeane nodded. "See, my birth mother was Deanie. Well, that's what they called her. Her mama named her Maudeane, but Mama refused to answer to it. I loved the idea of combining her name with Wilhelmina Worthington's, so that's what I did. I thought about it a long time before I did it, but then I figured, why not? There's nothing stopping me. So I did."

"I have a follow-up question," Julia said. "Other than DNA, how did you make the leap to deciding you were Simon Worthington's grandchild? Our records show his son Ben was unmarried and childless."

"Well, he wasn't," Willadeane said. "Ben is my father, and I can assure you that he was married to my mama more than nine months before I turned up."

Julia cut a glance toward Meredith. Apparently it was her turn to dive in to the topic.

"What proof can you offer of this marriage, Willadeane? Our assistant has already done an extensive search of legal marriages and has found none for Ben Worthington."

"Did she look in Canada?" Willadeane asked defensively. "Because that's where they got married."

"Why Canada?" Meredith asked.

"Mama was Canadian. Ben met her when he was running from the draft."

Julia's brows rose. "You're alleging Ben Worthington was a draft dodger."

"No, ma'am," she said. "I'm *telling* you that's what he was. His number came up in the spring of 1967, and he married Deanie Phillips from Vancouver in November. A year later, in December of 1968, they came back to Georgia, and Ben turned himself in. By January of '69 he was headed for Vietnam on a troop transport and my mama was living in a little house her in-laws provided for her on Lombard Street. Ben died in May, and I was born and then adopted by a family in Savannah. That was in August of 1969."

Meredith leafed through the file in front of her as she took in what the woman said. Indeed there were documents showing a marriage in Vancouver, a military record of Ben's service and death, and a certificate of a live birth for a female born August 25, 1969, at a Charleston hospital.

Meredith glanced at these documents then looked up at Willadeane. "There's no trace of a wife or child in his military records. That makes no sense."

"I don't know why either," she responded, seemingly nonplussed by the scrutiny of her story. "Although it could be because he wasn't married when he was first called up and he fled to Canada. When he came back, maybe nobody thought to change it."

"You seem to know a lot of information about your mother and father that wouldn't be found in a legal document," Julia said. "How did you learn all this?"

"Two years ago, I found my mother's sister through an ancestry site. She was living in Philadelphia and agreed to meet me. We became very close before she passed away last year. I've summarized what she told me in your packets, but the short version is that when Ben died, my mother took off."

"Why did she take off?"

"Auntie blamed Ben's uncle Thomas."

Julia shook her head. "I don't understand. What reason would Thomas have for rejecting Ben's wife and child? It seems like he would welcome Ben's child to keep his memory alive."

"Oh," Meredith said slowly, "I can think of one big reason. With Simon childless, the Worthington fortune would go to Thomas's children alone."

"Yes," Willadeane said. "Simon was adopted, but biologically he belonged to Daniel...."

"But not to Wilhelmina?" Julia asked. "Is that what you're saying? That would explain why Wilhelmina wanted the stipulation in the will that future heirs, in this case great-grandchildren, must be born to a legal marriage."

"Exactly," Willadeane said. "I don't know if you're interested, but Simon's mother was rumored to be Daniel's secretary, Bea Mills. Out of curiosity, I always planned to see what I could find out about her so I could add to my family tree. I just haven't had the time."

"All of the information you've just told us is documented in this packet?" Julia asked.

"It is, and I have more if you want it." She looked down at the table and then back up at Meredith then Julia. "Everything else is in my office. Say the word and I probably have a copy of it."

"About that DNA test," Meredith said, bringing the conversation back to the topic at hand. "Would you be willing to repeat it?"

Chapter Six

Julia met Meredith's gaze. Just yesterday they had discussed whether to have each potential heir take a DNA test. Julia's position was that it might be difficult to require a test from each prospective great-grandchild, that it might require a court order.

While Meredith agreed that it would likely be difficult to get each claimant to agree to a DNA test, she thought they should at least get the ones they could.

The way she saw it, with a percentage of a $100 million payout as incentive, any person who refused was probably not actually related anyway. Who in the world would argue against taking a test with that kind of reward for passing it?

Julia countered with points of law, and ultimately the two of them had agreed to at least explore the feasibility of testing. Basically, they would decide what to do if and when the situation arose.

"Absolutely. Now?" Willadeane asked without hesitation, ending any possible issue.

"No, not now," Meredith told her. "The law firm that represents Wilhelmina Worthington's estate will administer the test at its office."

"Fair enough. Just tell me where and when, and I'll be there."

Julia scribbled something on her notepad then looked up at Willadeane. "I'll have Carmen set up an appointment for you at Lucas, Wilson, Kyler & Strong."

"Today, if possible," Willadeane said.

Meredith sat back in her chair and smiled. "So you're anxious to get this done?"

"I am," she said. "But I know what the results will be, so if you mean anxious as in worrying, no. It would be helpful if I could go ahead and take the test today, though. It's hard to get away by myself, so I try to do everything I need to do at one time."

"I'm sorry if I'm prying, Willadeane," Meredith said, "but what is it that takes up so much of your time?"

She shrugged. "The sweetest elderly ladies you'd ever want to meet. All those years of taking care of Mama and Daddy gave me plenty of experience. It also showed me that not everyone has family ready or able to care for them. My parents would have loved to fill the rooms of the big house they left me with children, but that wasn't to be. So I got a nursing degree and filled those rooms with these ladies. We're classified as a hospice of sorts, and I just do what I can to be there for them as long as I have them."

"That's very admirable," Julia said. "It takes a special kind of person to do that sort of work, especially when it means opening your home to them."

"They're the special ones," she said. "So is there anything else you need from me?"

"I don't think so." Meredith looked over at Julia, who confirmed the statement with a shake of her head. "Just get the new DNA test done, and then we will be in touch."

"Thank you both." Willadeane stood, her eyes suddenly brimming with unshed tears. "I can't explain how good it feels to finally be taken seriously."

Julia snatched up another tissue and rose to hand it to her. "Come with me, Willadeane. I'll let Carmen know she needs to put you in touch with the law firm."

"Willadeane, wait," Meredith called as a thought occurred. "Out of curiosity, I have one more question, if you don't mind my asking. What do you plan to do with your share of the money if you are proven to be an heir?"

"Help my ladies," she said without hesitation. "And take more in. A bigger facility will mean more beds and more help for me. I don't want to get too big, because I still want to be hands on with my ladies. But if I moved my patients to a bigger facility, I might be able to open my home for caregivers to come and stay on respite. The sky's the limit if the funding is there. Just imagine how I could spoil my patients if I had the budget to do that."

Meredith smiled and stood to offer her goodbyes as the other two left the room. A few minutes later, Julia returned and closed the conference room door behind her.

"Thoughts?" Meredith asked, not willing to be the first to express her opinion of the woman they'd just interviewed.

"She seems sincere, and I can't help but be swayed to like her based on her last answer. I'm glad you asked that question, even if it isn't in the protocol for items we have to check off." Julia returned to her chair then swiveled to face Meredith. "I'm going to reserve my opinion about the validity of her claim until we receive the DNA results." She tucked the stack of papers Willadeane had given her beneath her legal pad. "I would like to revisit our conversation from our meeting yesterday."

"You mean about whether or not to require all claimants take a DNA test?" Meredith asked. "I can't imagine qualifying someone unless there's science behind it."

Julia shook her head. "I meant the other conversation where we listed the possible heirs."

"Yes, that one is safer," Meredith said with a chuckle. "What about it?"

"We're agreed that the other known heirs are the Worthington twins and Trey Worthington, all descendants through Wilhelmina's son Thomas. As of now there are no great-grandchildren qualified to inherit through Simon."

"Unless Willadeane's claim is proven by science, of course," Meredith told her.

"Which it might be. Only time will tell." Julia paused. "So there's nothing new in what you've taken home to read?"

"Nothing." Meredith shook her head. "Just a lot of fortune seekers. I got through half a box in one sitting. I'll finish the rest of it tonight and then send it back to Theo so his office can send them the 'thanks for playing' email. Tomorrow I'll bring another box home and continue the process."

"About that," Julia said. "I'm not sure I'm on board with responding in an email."

"We've been over that," Meredith said. "Theo's firm is good with it. Apparently, email is a viable way to reach people nowadays."

Julia shrugged. "I know, but I'm old school. I like my paper trails."

"That's fine." Meredith paused for effect. "How long do you think it'll take to communicate with all these opportunists, old-school style?"

Julia blew out a long breath and tucked a strand of hair behind her ear. "You've got a point. Plus, I always had a rule in my courtroom that the lawyers handled things and I only interjected my opinion when it was required. At this point, my opinion is not required."

"No, but your investigative skills are, and so are mine. Did Carmen get contact information for Kate and Kenneth?"

"I've got good news and bad news on that. Kate is obviously easy to find, even for someone who doesn't watch the weather on TV." She grinned at Meredith, then her expression sobered. "Her twin, Kenneth, is another story. Carmen found a lot about his antics and nothing about his location or how to contact him. I suggest starting with Kate in the hopes we can get information on him from her."

"What antics?" Meredith waved her hands. "Never mind. I don't need to know. We're only here to determine heirship and not to pass judgment on behavior."

"Thank goodness," Julia said.

"So back to heirs. According to public records, Simon had one child, Benjamin Henry Worthington, who was never married and died in Vietnam in 1969," Meredith said. "And that's where it ends."

"Again, unless you believe Willadeane's version," Julia offered.

"Look, I'll admit she's a nice lady. But we can't give a percentage of the trust to anyone based on being nice." She paused to look at her watch. "Why don't we see if we can catch Kate before she leaves the station?"

Julia rose and walked to the door to call to Carmen, and Meredith followed a step behind. "Would you see if you can get us an appointment with Kate Collins? She's the weather—"

"Ooh! I know her. She does the weather on WSVG," Carmen exclaimed. "You want me to tell her you're on your way, or do you prefer to get an appointment?"

"Tell her we're on our way," Meredith said. "And tell her it's an urgent matter regarding her great-grandmother, Wilhelmina Worthington."

Carmen gave the okay sign and reached for her phone while Meredith and Julia headed for the back door.

A few minutes later, Kate Collins met them in the studio's reception area wearing jeans, white sneakers, and a pale green sweater. Her hair had been pulled into a fashionable ponytail and the stage makeup she wore was gone. Off duty, Kate's fresh-scrubbed skin made her look much younger than the weather person on television.

She ushered them into a sunny office with a view of trees with the city just beyond. Two glass walls let in the light and warmed the space, which was just large enough for a brilliantly painted yellow desk and a small sofa covered in navy blue velvet and filled with pillows in a riot of colors. The two walls opposite the windows were painted a matching navy blue. Prestigious awards for forecasting and journalism vied for space among the silver-framed children's artwork that must have been done by Kate's children.

On her desk in a smaller silver frame was a family photograph. Tiny Kate, who had been on the gymnastics team in college, and her former University of Georgia fullback husband, Lamar Collins, stood on a beach with their three children—curly-haired twin boys of about six or seven and a beautiful daughter no more than age three—running in the surf behind them. It was the essence of summer and family all rolled up into one beautiful picture.

Meredith smiled when she caught Kate watching her. "You have a lovely family."

"Thank you." She let out a long breath. "I am blessed beyond measure, and I don't take that for granted. Where are my manners? Please, sit, won't you? Can I get you something to drink?"

Julia perched on one end of the sofa. "That won't be necessary. Thank you for seeing us on such short notice."

Meredith pushed some of the pillows out of the way and took a seat next to Julia while Kate turned the desk chair around and settled there. "We're just here to ask some questions, and then we'll get out of your way."

"It's no problem," Kate said. "Your assistant said it was urgent that you speak with me about my great-grandmother." She shrugged. "I have a little time before I'm supposed to join a friend for lunch, but I don't know how much help I'll be. She died before I was born, so I never knew her. My mother might be able to help, though."

"You're the one we need to speak with." Julia leaned forward, her hands resting on the black leather portfolio in her lap. "Magnolia Investigations has been tasked with verifying the list of heirs who will share in Wilhelmina Worthington's trust."

Kate's expression never changed. Obviously she knew this already. She crossed one leg over the other and rested her hand on the glassy surface of her desk. The massive stone that formed the centerpiece of her wedding ring glinted in the sunlight and cast a shower of tiny rainbows around the room. "I will be glad to help however I can. What is it you need from me?"

As they'd planned on the drive over, Julia opened her portfolio, retrieved her pen, and then took the lead. "Obviously, we are conducting a face-to-face meeting with you in order to verify you're alive and well. However, we're missing the contact information for your brother. Would you have that?"

Her smile went south, replaced by an unreadable look. Then, a moment later, the smile returned. "Kenneth isn't easy to find," she said. "I'm sure you know, but he makes a living with his skateboard, and that takes him all over the world."

"Yes, our assistant filled us in," Meredith said. "I understand he's quite good at what he does."

Kate shrugged. "When he's here in Savannah he generally stays in my pool house, unless he's on good terms with our mother—which is rare. On those occasions, he stays with her."

"That's helpful," Julia said, "but where is he now?"

She seemed to consider the question for a moment. "I don't know," she finally said. "And frankly, I don't care."

"I see." Julia paused. "Okay, then. We can check with your mother on that."

"Unfortunately, she won't know either." Kate's shoulders slumped. "Look, I'm sorry. We're twins. I should have more empathy for him, but I just don't. Kenneth rides around on a skateboard and refuses to grow up. He only contacts me or my mom if he needs something. He gets what he wants and then disappears. Meanwhile, I have three children who hardly even know what their only uncle looks like. We have very little in common anymore."

"I'm sorry," Meredith said. "That must be difficult."

"Kenneth is difficult," Kate corrected. "The whole situation is unfortunate, but my brother could easily fix it. He just doesn't want to." She shrugged. "I'm sorry. You didn't come here to listen to my complaints. I'll see if I can find him."

Julia retrieved a business card from her portfolio and handed it to Kate. "Just let us know. Meanwhile I wonder if you could give us your mother's contact information. She may have an insight that we don't know we need." She paused a second before continuing. "But only if you feel comfortable doing that. We can certainly reach out to her through other means."

"No, that's fine. For all the size of this city, Savannah is a small town. I know about you ladies and your reputation." Kate swiveled in her chair to open the desk drawer. She pulled out a business card. Turning it over, she grabbed a pen and began writing. "Here you go," she said, turning back to Julia when she was done.

"Thank you." Julia accepted the card and tucked it into her portfolio.

"Kate," Meredith said, "you obviously knew about the trust and that you might inherit. I suppose that means Kenneth knows too?"

"We were raised by a Worthington," Kate said. "So of course we both knew. And then there was Trey. He never stopped talking about it."

She seemed irritated and reluctant to continue. Meredith had the distinct feeling the meeting had just gone sour and they were about to be asked to leave.

Chapter Seven

"HAVE I SAID SOMETHING WRONG, Kate?" Meredith asked.

"No." Kate studied the silver pen in her hand. "My mom hardly ever talked about the trust. I mean, we had plenty, you know? But Trey? He was obsessed with what he would do when he got his share of the money. 'It's just the three of us' he would say. 'We'll get millions, and we can do whatever we want and never have to bow down to the mighty Worthingtons again.' Anytime I tried to talk to my mother about it, she refused to discuss it. If I nagged her about it, she'd snap and tell me I'd never see a penny of it. That Trey would get it all and Kenneth and I would get nothing."

"Why would she say that?" Julia asked. "You're an obvious heir through your father's birth."

"Who knows?" Kate's humor returned. "I imagine when my daughter's a teenager I'll get as frustrated with her as my mother got with me. I only know that she was probably trying to shut me up. I'm sure I deserved it. I was an obnoxious teenager on occasion."

"I had sons," Meredith said. "Two of them. And as much as I love them as adults, there were definitely times I would have likely told them anything to end a conversation I no longer wanted to be in."

"Yes, I remember Chase from school. Lamar and I saw him at a Bulldogs tailgate last year with Carter and his family. Carter's kids are absolutely adorable, by the way."

"Thank you. They are," Meredith agreed. "And perfect. Unlike their father and uncle."

They shared a laugh. Then the room fell silent.

"My next question was going to be about Trey," Julia said. "Do you know where your cousin is?"

Kate's chuckle held no humor. "I wish I did, but then again, I'm glad I don't, all at the same time. So the short answer to that is no."

"And do you know of anyone who might have that information?" Julia asked.

"Maybe his lawyer," she offered. "Do you need his name?"

"No, I already have a call in to him," Julia said. "I'll try again this afternoon. I left a voice mail asking him to return my call. I think the next one will say he must call Judge Foley on an urgent matter. Maybe that will get his attention. With attorneys, a call from a judge usually does."

The pair laughed, and Meredith seized the moment to ask a question of her own. "Kate, would you be willing to take a DNA test?"

"This would be totally voluntary, of course." Julia shot Meredith a warning look. Which Meredith promptly ignored.

"For what purpose?" Kate asked, her perfect brows gathering.

"To create a paper trail and verify what we already know," Meredith said. "That you're Wilhelmina Worthington's great-granddaughter."

"You don't have to answer now. Think about it and let us know," Julia added.

"No, it's fine," she said. "I'm just surprised. Is it a blood test or something?"

"Nothing that invasive," Meredith said. "It's a DNA test done with a saliva sample. The law firm handling the estate will administer the test in its office and deliver the results to us when they're in." She paused. "And to you as well, if you want to see them."

"Theo Lucas's firm?" Kate asked, and Meredith nodded. "Sure. No problem. I guess I need to call them and set it up. And yes, it would be fun to see the results. I've thought about getting kits for Lamar and me but haven't done it."

Julia handed her one of Theo's cards. "Thank you."

She took the card from Julia and examined it. "I guess I need to send this information to Kenny and tell him to get on it?"

"You can get in touch with him?" Meredith asked. Hadn't Kate just said she didn't know where her brother was?

Kate paused, her expression unreadable. Then she dipped her head and picked up her phone.

"Well, yes. I do have a cell phone number. I just don't know where in the world he's located. Did you want that number?" She looked up, her smile back in place. "I assumed you needed a physical location to send documents or I would have offered before."

Ron had taught Meredith to look past a person's words to his or her expression and body language. Unless Meredith missed her guess, there was more to the story than Kate was telling them.

"Yes," Meredith said. "We need to speak with him and verify everything."

"He's my twin. If I'm verified, then I'm pretty sure that verifies him too, even though we're obviously fraternal twins." She shrugged. "But I'll be glad to give you his number. Can I text it to you?"

Meredith gave Kate her number, and a moment later her phone dinged with a text. She looked down to find the twin's contact card. "Skate? That's his nickname, right?"

Kate sighed. "Yes. He's been Skate Worthington since junior high. I don't call him that anymore but haven't bothered to change it in my contact list. Anyway, that's way more information than you've asked for or need to know about my brother."

"Thank you for the phone number," Julia said. "Do you have any questions for us before we go?"

"Before we get to that," Meredith interjected, "would you mind answering one more question for me, Kate, just out of personal curiosity?"

"Sure, what is it?"

"What will you do with your part of the trust if you're named as an heir to your great-grandmother Worthington's trust?"

Kate paused only a second. "Get better seats at the Georgia Bulldog games, I guess. And maybe set something aside to help the kids go to college." She shrugged. "There can't be that much there, and I have to share it with Trey and my brother. I mean, Mama heard that Grandma Wilhelmina was crazy. Did you know they had to put her away?"

"We did not," Julia said, obviously shocked.

"Well, that's according to my mother, who heard it from my grandfather, her father-in-law. Evidently, Wilhelmina got so mad at them that she changed her will and that was the end of that. No one would touch the money for two generations. That way none of her sons would live to see the money distributed—or so Mama said."

"So that's the reason," Meredith said. "I guess I see her point, but that's rather extreme."

"Thomas and Simon were out and so were their children." Kate paused. "Of course none of that would have been made public during all those years the will was held up in court, what with the gag order on. I can't tell you how hard it was, even as the weather forecaster, to work at a news station and know newsworthy information but not be able to give my colleagues the scoop on what was really going on and why Wilhelmina Worthington cut her family out."

Meredith considered how to respond. "Why do you assume there isn't much in the trust?"

Kate turned toward her. "When she went into the loony bin, she allegedly released control of everything she owned over to her husband, Daniel, and her sons. Daniel died less than a year later. If the money ever got put back into an account that Wilhelmina could get her hands on, such information never filtered down the family tree to my parents. Mama swears the old lady only had what her husband left her, and that went to Thomas when she died."

"Well, Meredith and I have taken up enough of your time with our questions," Julia said. "Thank you again for agreeing to meet with us on short notice."

Kate rose when they did. "Do you have any idea when all of this will be settled?"

"There's no timetable," Julia said. "Although we are hoping to get it done quickly."

"Oh good," Kate said, relief crossing her face.

"Why?" Julia asked.

"Because tickets go on sale in another month or so for next season. If Lamar and I are going to get better seats, we need to start talking about how much we're willing to spend and where in the stadium we want to sit."

"Of course." Julia slanted a glance over in Meredith's direction. Her expression confirmed that Julia had much less appreciation for the intricacies of Georgia Bulldog season tickets than Meredith and Kate did.

Meredith gathered up her purse. "You don't have to see us out. We'll find the way—"

Someone knocked at the door and then it flew open. Harper Finch stepped inside. Of average height with a dark bob and dark eyes, Harper had gone to school with Carter, and even back then she was sticking her nose where it didn't belong. That talent had served her well, for she'd been in the employ of *Savannah Morning News* for the better part of two decades.

"Hey, Kate, are you ready to go to lunch?" Harper asked. "Oh. Mrs. Bellefontaine, Judge Foley, I'm sorry. I didn't realize Kate had anyone with her. Are you here at the station to be interviewed?"

"No," they said in unison.

"Actually, we were just leaving," Meredith told her as she edged toward the door. "Do give my best to your mother."

"Mama's in Palm Beach until after Thanksgiving, but I'll pass on the message when I see her." Harper took a tiny step into the space between Meredith and the exit. "It doesn't take an investigative reporter to guess you're here about the Worthington excitement. What's the latest on that situation?"

"We can't say," Julia stated firmly. "You'll have to speak to Theo Lucas about any questions you've got in that regard."

Harper shook her head. "Theo is almost as tight-lipped as Kate about this subject. I know she can't tell me things because of her family connections and all, but you'd think that the attorney who's working on the estate would want to be friendly to the media."

"Why?" Meredith asked.

Harper affected an innocent look. "Sometimes we get tips on things. A little cooperation goes a long way, you know."

"Let it go, Harper," Kate said, her tone firm but gentle. "You're putting them on the spot, and they don't have any more freedom to give interviews than I do."

Harper shrugged. "A good investigative reporter tries to get the story anyway."

"Well, thank you for making time for us today, Kate." Julia pressed past Meredith and Harper and out of the office. "We'll be in touch if we have any more questions."

Meredith offered a smile to Kate and then winked. "Yes, thank you. Let me know if your current football tickets go up for sale."

Kate stifled a grin. "I will."

"What was that about?" Meredith heard Harper say just before Kate closed the door.

"What was that indeed," Julia muttered. "I don't like being cornered, especially by a reporter."

"She was just doing her job," Meredith said as they stepped out into the sunshine. "But I'm with you. I don't like it either."

Julia clicked the button to unlock her car and they climbed inside. "We're going to have to do something about these reporters, Meredith. We cannot keep getting ambushed like that. Between the ones who showed up the first day we met with Theo to today's incident, like it or not we are now in the public eye."

"We have been before," Meredith said. "We just need to have a plan. Other than referring everyone to Theo."

"Which we will continue to do," Julia said as she shifted the car into REVERSE. "I do not intend to speak to anyone from the press about this case. I think from now on we just say a firm 'no comment' and move on."

Meredith thought about that for a moment. Finally she nodded. "Yes, I think that's the only way. If we say anything, we're just going to give them something to write about."

Her phone buzzed, and she looked down to see it was a text from Quin. She'd found it necessary to cancel plans with him the other night in order to make her way through the box of Worthington documents she'd brought home. He'd seemed to take the last-minute cancellation well but hadn't rescheduled.

Touching the icon, Meredith waited a moment until the text appeared. DINNER WITH ME, OR WITH ANOTHER BOX FROM WORK?

She must have made a face, because Julia glanced over in her direction. "Something wrong?"

Meredith tucked her phone away. "No. Just a text from Quin asking about dinner."

Julia kept her silence as she turned the corner. When they were stopped at a light, she looked over again. "I thought you enjoyed spending time with him. Why the face?"

"I do." She shrugged. "I think it's this case. It's a big responsibility to name these heirs, and I'm not taking it lightly."

"I'm not either," Julia said. "But I don't see what that has to do with having the occasional dinner with Quin."

"It should have nothing to do with it," Meredith said. "But it does. We've given every case our all ever since we opened, but rarely have I gone home at night and felt like I didn't do enough during the day on anything we've investigated. Since the boxes came, I've been taking them home and staying up until the wee hours of the morning reading contact forms from Theo's office."

"Meredith," Julia said, "I hope I haven't made you feel as though you had to do that."

"No, of course not. This pressure is something I've put on myself. You've had nothing to do with it."

Julia sighed. "Well, I feel terrible adding this to your burden, but I was about to ask if you wanted to go to the diner and meet with Charlene and Maggie Lu to finalize the details for Clarissa's baby shower on the twenty-first. I can go alone."

Meredith groaned. "Oh no. I completely forgot about the baby shower. I haven't done a single thing to help on that." She reached down by her feet to retrieve her purse and then pulled out the pocket-sized leather notebook with attached silver pen that Carter had given her for Mother's Day. "Remind me what I was supposed to do, and I'll do it this afternoon. I promise."

"Meredith, relax," Julia said. "Carmen has been handling everything. We're just finalizing the menu." She chuckled. "Charlene knows what her daughter likes, but Maggie Lu gets the final approval. It won't surprise you to hear that mother and daughter may be bumping heads on what to serve. Charlene asked if we would come by after the lunch crowd is over and act as the tiebreaker."

"That sounds dangerous," Meredith said. "I wouldn't want to cross either of them. But no, you don't have to go alone."

"Are you sure?"

"Yes, I'm sure. I just need to loosen up a little about the Worthington case. We know what we're doing, and everything will be fine." She paused. "I also should forget about bringing a box home tonight and accept a dinner date with a handsome man."

"Yes to all of that," Julia said. "Now, the question is, do we grab a snack before we go over to the diner or wait until we get there to eat? It may be two o'clock before Charlene calls to let us know she's ready for us."

"Are you kidding?" Meredith said. "Charlene's food is worth the wait. Let's go back to the office. I'll relieve my guilt by going through contact forms until it's time to leave."

"I agree. And while you're reading those forms, I'll check back with my friend in New York to see if he's made any headway into the question of where Trey Worthington might be, if he's still living." She paused. "Oh, and we need to have Carmen set up an appointment with Kate's mother."

Meredith nodded. "Should we wait until we meet with her before we try to contact Kate's twin, Kenneth?"

"Maybe," Julia said. "The last thing we need to do is frighten him off if he's prone to hiding like Kate said. My question, though, is who is Kenneth Worthington hiding from and why?"

"I think Kate knows." Meredith paused. "But remember, we aren't supposed to be doing anything except qualifying heirs. Whatever he's up to, if it isn't related to that, then it is out of the scope of our investigation."

"That doesn't keep me from being curious," Julia protested. "But I'm sure we'll find out what we need to know from his mother."

"Sunny Worthington's wedding to Chip Conrad IV in 1993 was the most ostentatious wedding I've ever attended. Twenty-four bridesmaids, Julia, and three days of festivities in three different counties plus a bridesmaid's luncheon at the Plaza Hotel in New York City that made all the society columns. Can you imagine?"

"I cannot." She signaled to turn left. "But I would imagine the Worthingtons always did things on a grand scale."

"I'll say," said Meredith. "I remember Wilhelmina's funeral. There were more flowers there than any ten funerals I've ever seen." She gathered her purse and phone. "Do you remember that?"

Julia eased into her parking space and turned off the engine. "That was the summer I was working two jobs to save for law school." She gave Meredith a wry grin. "I think I missed that one."

The fact that Meredith and her best friend had very different starts in life rarely came up in conversation anymore. Scrappy Julia had made her own way in the world, rising to the position of judge by her own hard work. In contrast, Meredith had been handed much of what she received, though she had never shied away from the efforts it took to succeed.

Meredith reached for the door handle. "You're absolutely my hero, Julia. What you went through to get where you are is what makes you so good at what you do. Anyone else would have given up."

"Give up?" Julia grinned and stepped out of the car then looked at Meredith over the roof of her vehicle. "Where would be the fun in that?"

Chapter Eight

"Of all the ways Daniel Worthington could have died, it figures he would manage to make a mess from the front door all the way to my bedroom."

Theo did not even bother to look surprised as he set his newspaper aside and glanced over toward the door. Only then did she see there were two cups of coffee on his desk. One for him and one for her.

Wilhelmina smiled. Of course he'd known the first place she would come on the morning after her husband had been found dead was here.

She looked down at the newspapers as she closed the distance between them. "Did any of them get the story right?"

"That depends," Theo said in that slow way he had of talking when he was trying to get someone to take over the conversation. "What's the story?"

She'd been practicing the answer to this question for hours. Longer than that, if the truth was known. Which it wouldn't be. Not outside this room, anyway.

"*Unfortunately, Daniel is dead. End of story.*"

"*Then they got it right.*" *Theo leaned back in his chair and watched her settle across from him. "Only thing I can't figure is why the Aubusson carpet in your room was soaking wet.*"

"*Who knows?*" *Wilhelmina let that question hang in the air between them as she sipped the hot brew.*

Theo was correct. Wilhelmina had found Daniel slumped over in the shower with his life draining away faster than the warm water still pouring over him. Out of respect for the man he once was, she couldn't let him be seen like that by strangers.

She'd left him to call an ambulance, but he'd called for her before she got three steps into the bedroom. "Don't leave me," he'd said in a voice thick with what must have been pain.

Here it was. Her chance to show him the back of her as she ignored his dying wish and sashayed out of the room. Her chance to pay him back for every pain he'd inflicted, not with his hands but with his actions.

But she was a fool. A sentimental old fool. And she had loved the man he'd been when she married him. The man she wished he still was.

So she stayed with him.

She fell on her knees, with the water from the shower flowing around them, and held Daniel in her arms. It only lasted a moment or two, and then he gasped and offered the world his last breath before quietly slipping on to the next one.

She'd used the rug to drag him to the bedroom and then managed to get him dried, dressed, and into bed before she reached for the phone. Who did one call in a situation like this? In the moment, she had no idea. So Wilhelmina did what she always did when she wasn't sure who was supposed to handle a problem. What she'd done her entire life.

She rang for the maid.

"Did you do it?" Theo asked, his gaze unwavering. "I can only get you acquitted if you're honest with me. That stunt he pulled when he tried to get you committed would be suffi-cient grounds."

She barely blinked. "No."

He didn't move a muscle as he continued to watch her. "Do you know who did?"

That awful woman who followed Ben home from Canada came to mind. She'd certainly been a taxation on Daniel's heart and disposition. No, Daniel had handled that situation and they'd never heard from her again.

Then there was the very public spat with Thomas at the board meeting earlier in the week. Since neither of them confided in her, the news of their falling out had landed on her ears in the usual way: from her beautician at her weekly appointment.

"Not with any certainty, no," Wilhelmina finally said.

Bushy brows rose, but Theo said nothing. Wilhelmina took another sip of coffee then placed the cup back on the desk in front of her.

She'd worn a Chanel houndstooth suit from last year's col-lection this morning, not because she liked it but because the fabric was mostly black and the netting on the matching pillbox hat covered what her oversized sunglasses did not. If anyone recognized her—which Wilhelmina hoped they would not—she would look like what she was: a woman in mourning.

Not that she was mourning Daniel Worthington. She'd miss him, to be sure, but the man Wilhelmina thought she had married had died and been mourned long ago.

The death she was mourning today was the death of her privacy. Of her ability to stop all conversation in a room because of how she looked or what she was wearing rather than because they were all gossiping about her. Even her stint in the looney bin back in the sixties hadn't caused her this kind of consternation.

But then Theo had covered that up nicely. This time around, there was nothing Theo could do.

Wilhelmina shrugged off the thought and focused her attention on her reason for being there. "Did he leave me anything?"

"I'm not his attorney anymore, Willa," he said gently. "I haven't been for over a decade now, and you know that."

"But you know who is," she said, ignoring the jab at her forgetfulness, which was happening far too often to suit her these days. "And if I know you, you've already anticipated my question and placed a discreet call that neither of you would admit to."

The corners of Theo's eyes crinkled as the beginning of a smile rose. "A life estate in the home where you now reside, a trust with your name on it, and the key to a safe-deposit box."

So Daniel had not made good on his claim to toss her out of the home that was owned by the corporation. Apparently he cared how he looked to the community, even after death.

"How much is in the trust?" she asked.

"One dollar. His lawyer said you would know why."

One dollar. Yes, she knew why.

"I told him more than once that I missed the Daniel I married back when he only had a dollar to his name. I sure loved that man back then."

Theo ducked his head, his expression somber. When he lifted his head again, he reached into his desk drawer and pulled out a small key and a brown envelope slightly smaller than a recipe card. Without a word, he slid both across the table toward Wilhelmina.

A stamp across the middle indicated that the envelope was the property of Savannah National Bank. She turned it over and saw that the envelope was sealed shut.

"Just donate that dollar to your favorite charity, would you, Theo?" she said as she dropped the key into her handbag and rose. "And in case you're wondering how Daniel managed to ruin the carpet, it was indirectly. Once the emergency call went out, we had half of Savannah's first responders on our doorstep and inside the house. While I appreciate their professionalism, I do wish they would have wiped their boots first."

He looked relieved. "That does make sense."

She let out a long breath. "Daniel's death was unfortunate. He worked too much, ate all the wrong things, stayed mad at somebody most of the time, and refused to do *anything about any of this. I begged Thomas to join me in trying to get him to take care of himself. He ignored me and said his dad would live forever and we should let him be."*

"Typical sentiment of those who don't yet have sore backs and poor sleep habits," Theo quipped. "People are talking already, Willa. Prepare to defend him and yourself better than you have with me. You'll do yourself no favors if you don't."

Wilhelmina waved away the statement. "Ignore the rumors, Theo. Thomas loved his father. As for me, there's nothing to defend. Anyone who knew Daniel well knew what I put up with and that I stayed with him anyway. They know neither of us wanted him dead."

Gone, maybe, but not dead. *A thought. Never a statement she would make.*

"Would you like to make a statement to the press?" He paused. "I'll be glad to handle that for you."

"Daddy always said I ought never to miss an opportunity to keep my mouth shut. I think I'll take his advice, at least for now," she said. "But thank you, Theo. I'll let you know if I change my mind."

She almost got to the door before Theo called her name. She turned to find him watching her.

"Who punched the coroner, Willa?"

Wilhelmina let that question hang in the air between them for a moment. She hadn't worn gloves just because they went with the suit. She'd be wearing them until the bruises healed.

There would be no crime reported, because the coroner would never admit he was hit by a woman. She barely *admitted it to herself. Never in her life had she raised a hand to a man. But this one deserved it for the words he'd said. The allegations he'd made.*

She shook her head.

"How about that?" Wilhelmina said with a well-practiced smile. "I get to take Daddy's advice twice in one morning and it's not yet eight o'clock. Do have a good day, Theo. I'll let you know when the funeral arrangements are formalized."

She left her lawyer's office the same way she'd arrived, through the back door. The bank wouldn't be open for an hour, but she couldn't go home. Not yet.

So Wilhelmina got into the gleaming white 1971 Cadillac Eldorado convertible that had been delivered just last week—Daniel had insisted she get a new one every year—removed her pillbox hat, and replaced it with the dark sunglasses and yellow floral silk scarf she kept in the glove compartment.

Then she backed the car out of the parking lot, turned onto the street that ran alongside Forsyth Park, and drove. She wasn't headed anywhere in particular, and yet she knew she was going where she was supposed to go.

Somehow she ended up in front of the dingy little house on Lombard Street that she and Daniel had lived in when they were first married. Wilhelmina pulled the Cadillac to a stop in front and turned off the engine. Silence fell, punctuated by the chirp of birds in the towering oak tree she and Daniel had planted as a seedling.

They still owned the place, at least as far as she knew. Daniel probably rented it out or had loaned it out to an employee in need. For all his faults, he did have a soft heart when it came to just about everyone but family.

She looked past the neatly trimmed yard and the starched lace curtains to the little child watching her from the window of the room where she'd first placed Thomas in his crib. Papa had thought she was crazy to move in here with Daniel when he'd offered to buy her the grandest house in town and an allowance to furnish it however she wished.

But Wilhelmina hadn't wanted a grand home with all the trappings of wealth. She hadn't wanted the Chanel suits and a gleaming new white Cadillac convertible every year. All she'd wanted—or needed—was Daniel's love.

Only then, with that realization, did she finally cry.

A light flashed, and she gasped. When her vision cleared, a man with a camera stood next to another fellow who was already putting pen to paper.

"Mrs. Worthington!" he called as he crossed the street halfway then stopped to allow a delivery truck and several cars to pass.

Oh no. No.

Wilhelmina ignored him, swiping at the ridiculous tears the oversized sunglasses could not conceal with the corner of her scarf then reached to fumble with the keys. She should never have come here. Never should have shown her face on the streets of Savannah until she was ready for her face to be photographed.

"Mrs. Worthington! A moment of your time, please," he called again.

The keys fell from her trembling fingers and landed at her feet. She scrambled to find them, her perfectly manicured nails scraping plush carpet and cold metal before she finally scooped them up.

Once again the flashbulb went off. The convertible top that had offered freedom minutes ago now imprisoned her, making it impossible to ignore the reporter pressing closer with every step, the photographer shadowing him.

The Cadillac's big engine roared to life. In one swift motion, Wilhelmina shifted the car into DRIVE *and shot off from the curb like a bullet fired from Daddy's old hunting rifle.*

In the moment, all she could think of was getting away. Of avoiding any contact with reporters, men with cameras, or anyone who wanted to talk to her about the death of Daniel Worthington.

Only later, when she was convinced the reporter and his associate were not going to give pursuit, did she slow down and consider that she hadn't bothered to look before she pulled out onto that busy street. How she managed to escape without slamming into an oncoming car was beyond her. Only the Lord could have orchestrated such an exit.

He must have plans for her yet, though what those plans might be was also a mystery. She would solve that one another day.

Wilhelmina pulled into the garage behind the home she'd just been given a lifetime ownership of, courtesy of her husband's will, and turned off the engine. Her fingers still shook. Her heart still pounded. Tears still flowed.

She yanked off her scarf and mopped at her face, no longer caring if she smudged her makeup. Leaning against the headrest, Wilhelmina closed her eyes and held the scarf wadded against her cheek.

Clear as day, she heard her Daddy's voice. You're a stronger woman than you think you are. Always were. Always will be.

It wasn't him, of course. Logic told her this was her imagination.

Wilhelmina might have been accused of needing to be institutionalized, but she hadn't qualified for it yet.

"No I'm not, Daddy," she whispered. *"Not even close."*

Chapter Nine

AT A QUARTER PAST TWO, Meredith stepped into the Downhome Diner with Julia on her heels. The delicious smells of the lunch service still hung in the air, making her stomach growl.

Decorated like a fifties diner with booths and bright colors, the fare here was more than a cut above. It was one of Meredith and Julia's favorite places to eat.

Meredith spotted Maggie Lu King seated in a corner booth, sipping iced tea. When their dear friend spied them, she grinned and then waved.

Once they'd dispensed with their greetings all around, Julia and Meredith settled into the booth to await their other hostess. "Thank you for waiting until after the lunch crowd was gone," Maggie Lu said.

"Your daughter's food is always worth the wait. Are you getting excited about this great-grandbaby?" Julia asked her.

"As excited as an old lady can get," she said as she clapped her hands. "I didn't think there was anything greater than a grandbaby, but now that a great-grandbaby's set to make an appearance next month, I must concede I just might be wrong."

"Have Clarissa and Phillip found out if it's a boy or a girl yet?" Meredith asked as she took a sip of the iced tea the waitress delivered.

"Oh no," Maggie Lu said with a swipe of her hand. "None of that finding out ahead of time nonsense for them. They've decided they're going to be old school and be surprised. Imagine that. Something we did is catching on again. I guess that makes this old lady stylish."

"Did you tell her that?" Julia teased.

"I did. Clarissa thought it was funny." Maggie Lu glanced up. "Oh, there's my girl, and look what she's bringing us to eat."

Meredith followed Maggie Lu's gaze toward the kitchen and saw Charlene Jackson, the owner of Downhome Diner, heading toward them with a smile on her face and a pitcher of iced tea in her hand. Behind Charlene was a parade of waitresses, each carrying a tray laden with food. A young man, who looked more like a cook than a waiter, hurried ahead of them with three small folding tables.

When the parade reached the table, the young man hastily set up the folding tables nearby and the waitresses deposited the trays there.

Julia groaned. "Is all of that for us? I don't know whether to celebrate when I think of how delicious it'll taste or cry when I think of the calories I'll have to walk off on the treadmill."

"Don't think about calories," Maggie Lu said. "You're still young enough to just enjoy." She patted Charlene's hand and then affected a serious expression. "All right now, ladies. We are tasked with an important job, and I don't want any of you to take this lightly."

The reminder of the other task, the other important job she'd just been speaking to Julia about a few hours ago, arose. Meredith shook off the thought with a roll of her shoulders and then reached for a napkin.

"As Mama has already told you, we've had a hard time deciding what to feed our guests at the baby shower. My daughter has been absolutely no help, because she wants us to surprise her. So, that leaves us to make the decision."

Julia surveyed the trays and then shook her head as she returned her attention to Charlene. "Charlene, you've outdone yourself. I do not know how you stay so thin. I'm gaining weight just looking at that food."

Charlene grinned from ear to ear as she set the tea pitcher on the table and slid into the booth beside her mother. "Thank you. I had a great time coming up with these menus. It isn't our usual diner fare, but then it isn't every day I get to cook for a baby shower for my grandchild." She flushed pink. "My grandchild. Just saying that makes me want to tear up. I am so excited."

"We both are," Maggie Lu agreed. "The birth of a child is always such a grand blessing, but this just seems twice as sweet."

"Don't say that, Mama," Charlene exclaimed. "You know twins run in Philip's family, and my poor baby is as big as a house. There could definitely be two in there. Twice as sweet means twice the work, not that I wouldn't love to have twice the grandbabies."

"Wouldn't they tell you that at the doctor's office?" Maggie Lu asked. "Or at least tell the mama and the daddy. Give them a little advanced warning, maybe?"

"They would have," Charlene agreed. "But either my daughter is too stubborn to tell us we need to be preparing for two or she isn't having a double blessing this time around."

They shared a laugh, and then Maggie Lu raised her hand for attention. "All right now, ladies. Let's begin. Julia and Meredith, you know why you're here. I will defer to my daughter for the rules of the meal."

Charlene smiled. "Thank you, Mama. Each of the meals has been designated with a letter. So as you're served you'll be deciding on whether to choose Meal A, Meal B, or Meal C." She nodded to a waitress who had remained nearby. "Go ahead and serve Meal A, Annette."

"Do we need to have scorecards?" Meredith asked as she eyed the food being placed in front of her. "I'm pretty sure I'm going to love all of this and be completely useless in making a choice."

An hour later they had tried three amazing menus and were no closer to deciding which of the meals should be served at the baby shower on the twenty-first. Meredith leaned back against her seat and groaned.

"Charlene, I am absolutely stuffed. And I'm useless. I want all of it."

Julia laughed. "Me too, although I am partial to your fried chicken."

"Thank you," she said. "It's Mama's recipe. I just tweaked it a little. Do you think the ladies would like it? I mean, it isn't too heavy to serve at a luncheon, is it?"

"Gracious no," Meredith said. "Not with the cucumber salad and greens you paired it with."

"I think I'll offer both fried and grilled chicken just in case," Charlene said. "Ooh, grilled with a citrus glaze."

She went on to describe what could only be termed a heavenly meal. Meredith groaned again. "I couldn't eat another bite, but I am craving some of that grilled chicken now. For tomorrow's dinner," she quickly added.

"I think it's settled," Maggie Lu said. "Now we have to decide on the cake."

A chorus of groans followed her declaration. "I thought I could send three different pieces home with each of you and let you decide. Would that work?"

"That would be perfect," Julia said. "Do you mind if I take pieces big enough to share with Beau? He loves cake."

"I'll be happy to add extra pieces of cake for him too. The more opinions the better. I'm trying another of Mama's recipes—a hummingbird cake—so I am anxious for feedback."

"Did you mess with my hummingbird cake recipe?" Maggie Lu demanded in mock anger. "Your great-grandmother would have my hide for letting you get away with that."

Charlene glanced over at Julia and Meredith and winked. "Until I hear that from her, I'm going to assume my great-grandmother would have liked my version just fine."

"I sure raised a sassy daughter," Maggie Lu said.

"I turned out just like my mama," was Charlene's swift retort before she leaned over and kissed Maggie Lu on the cheek.

"Meredith, would you like one or two pieces of each?" Charlene asked as she rose.

"She would like two," Julia answered for her.

"Two?" Maggie Lu said. "Do tell."

"According to Julia, I have been working too hard. She's made me promise to take tonight off and enjoy it with Quin. He asked about dinner, but I think cake and coffee is about all I'll be able to manage." She paused. "So yes, two pieces of each, please."

Julia's gaze met hers. Her friend's eyes beamed.

"Meanwhile, I'll text Quin and let him know we're skipping dinner and going straight to dessert." She chuckled. "He may want to grab a sandwich first."

"No need to do that," Charlene said. "I'll throw in a nice meal for him too. Can't have that man trying to subsist on cake."

Meredith tried to protest, but Charlene ignored her efforts.

Finally she gave up. "You win, Charlene. Thank you."

Meredith dashed off a quick text to Quin as Charlene hurried off to take care of the cake orders.

"I understand you've taken on a big case," Maggie Lu said. "Sorting out the Worthington heirs will be a challenging job."

"Why do you say so?" Meredith asked, realizing Maggie Lu might have memories of the Worthington family and the mystery surrounding Daniel Worthington's death.

"Anything to do with the Worthingtons comes with its own set of challenges." She paused. "I remember her, you know. Wilhelmina Worthington was something, I'll tell you what. She drove around Savannah in a long white Cadillac convertible looking like she was Jackie Kennedy come to town. She was a sight indeed. Got a brand-new Cadillac every year, she did. At least until her husband died. Once he was gone, she kept the last one he gave her until she died. Some thought she'd have the funeral director dig the hole out at Bonaventure Cemetery big enough to bury her in that Caddy. Last I heard it was put away in storage and preserved. Who knows if that's true or not, though."

"Oh my," Julia said. "She does sound like a character."

"I believe it was 1977 when she finally passed, though I swear to you she drove that Cadillac to the beauty shop two days before she went home to Jesus. Funeral was something. Her son Simon and grandson Ben were already long gone by then—Simon died of the flu back in '60 or '61, I think, and his son Ben died in Vietnam. I think Ben must have been killed around '69. Such a pity. Thomas, he ordered every white rose in Georgia sent in for his mother's service. There were so many flowers, you could hardly breathe in the church for the scent of them."

"I was just telling Julia about that earlier," said Meredith.

"It sounds like Thomas really loved his mother," Julia said.

"He did, even if she cut him and his children out of her will," Meredith added as she put her phone away.

"Well now, it's funny you say that," Maggie Lu said. "If you think about it, that old woman sure knew how to hold a grudge. She was so mad at her husband and boys that she decided they wouldn't live to see the day her money went to any of their kin."

"We'd been told that," Meredith said. "We're working on proving it."

Maggie Lu gave her a look. "Have you talked to Amy? Now she goes by Willadeane Worthington."

Meredith looked over at Julia then back at Maggie Lu. "We've spoken with Willadeane."

"Then you know all about the situation," their friend said.

"We know what Willadeane has told us." Julia paused. "But there's nothing proving her claim yet. She's got DNA results, but we've asked her to repeat the testing through a more controlled procedure. Once those results come back, we will have a clearer picture of whether she's telling the truth. Why do you think she's an heir?"

Meredith studied their friend. "Maggie Lu, what is it you know that we ought to find out?"

"She's an heir, Meredith. I know it to be true." Maggie Lu shook her head. "Her mama was so young and all alone. I can't think of her now without thinking of how grateful I am to have people who care about me in my life. She didn't have that, once Ben was gone."

The diner was empty at the moment, and the crew was in the back, preparing for the evening shift. Still Meredith found herself looking around to make certain no one was listening.

"You knew Willadeane Worthington's birth mother?" Meredith asked.

"Yes, I knew her. There was a time in the late sixties after my husband died when I did alterations to help make ends meet. Teaching didn't pay much back then, and I was new on top of that. That's how we met." Maggie Lu took a sip of iced tea and then held the glass in front of her, swirling the ice in the amber liquid. She appeared to be lost in thought. "Daniel did wrong, but there was a lot of wrong to go around in that situation."

"Daniel?" Meredith shook her head. "I thought you were talking about Ben's daughter."

"I am," she said. "It's all just so complicated."

"Anything you could tell us would be helpful," Julia said. "We don't want to exclude anyone who might be a rightful heir."

Maggie Lu nodded. "Yes, I can see that. And I can also see your dilemma. Like it or not, you've got to play devil's advocate with any stranger who claims a relation to the family."

"Unfortunately, we do," Meredith said. "But I'm with Julia. If you can help us, we would be grateful."

"I can tell you the story," she said, a sad tone in her voice. "How much help it will be, I don't know."

Chapter Ten

MAGGIE LU PAUSED TO TAKE a sip of her iced tea. Then she continued. "When I met Deanie, she was already four or five months along. She needed to have some dresses let out, so I did that for her."

"And you became friends?" Meredith supplied.

"Not at first. She was not yet twenty and scared as a rabbit in an unfamiliar city with no family, as you can imagine. She'd said her goodbyes to Ben—he'd gotten into some trouble over his draft card status and had been shipped off to war—and she was all alone in that house Daniel put them in over on Lombard Street."

"That must have been difficult for her," Julia said. "But she had family in the Worthingtons, didn't she? Tommy Two would have been about her age." She paused. "But he was drafted too, I assume, and not there."

Maggie Lu shook her head. "Oh no," she said. "Thomas Worthington Sr.'s sons didn't get drafted. He saw to that. He'd sat out World War II on some kind of deferment thanks to his daddy, Daniel. Although Simon defied Daniel and enlisted to serve in the army."

"But Ben got drafted," Meredith protested.

She looked at them with sad eyes. "Getting drafted and actually going to war were two different things back then. His grandaddy gave him a way out. When the deferments didn't work, Daniel put his grandson on a plane to Canada before the draft board could catch up to him. Ben just couldn't stick to it. That boy was an honest man. A good man. He stayed in Canada just long enough to fall in love with Deanie, and then he came home to make things right." She paused again. "Plus he worried about his mama. Mary Worthington was a widow, and she'd never been particularly close to her in-laws."

"That sounds like a recurring theme," Julia quipped.

"So Willadeane is likely telling the truth?" Meredith asked. "How about that?"

"She is," Maggie Lu corrected. "If the person you talked to is, indeed, Willadeane Worthington, that is, but the DNA test will answer that. I'm the one who sewed baby clothes for her. I even made a ruffled yellow dress and a little stuffed doll as a gift for her because Deanie swore she was having a girl."

"So you were friends. Maybe you can tell us this," Julia said. "Instead of relying on her husband's very wealthy family to help her raise her child, why did Deanie give birth at a hospital in Charleston, give up her baby for adoption, and then disappear? Not having a good relationship is one thing, but disappearing is another. And giving your baby up? I cannot imagine."

Maggie Lu sat back and toyed with her tea glass for a moment, seemingly lost in thought. Then she looked up at Julia. "I'd say she was afraid."

"Of what?" Julia blurted out. "I don't understand."

"I don't either," Maggie Lu told her. "But she never much cared for Daniel Worthington. I always suspected he was behind her disappearance. No one in the Worthington family ever acknowledged that the baby had been born. Deanie's ninth month passed and there was nothing but silence. You've lived in Savannah long enough to know that when a society child comes into the world, there is a whole lot of hoopla that goes with welcoming the little one, before and after."

"Yes there is," Meredith said. "Didn't she tell you she was leaving?"

"She did not," Maggie Lu said. "One evening after work I went to that little house she was living in to drop off Ben's christening gown from when he was a baby. She was having me add lace trim and pearl buttons to it. Even though we'd arranged to meet that night, the place was empty. She'd left without a trace. I always thought it was odd, because I cannot imagine that she would leave without that christening gown."

"What did you do with it?" Julia asked.

"I gave it back to the family," she said. "I wrapped it up and took it over to the Worthington place, thinking that maybe Deanie had patched things up with her husband's people and moved in to the big house to wait for the baby to come."

"But she hadn't?" Julia offered.

"No. Ms. Effie Wilson, the cook, said so, and I believe her. Her mama and mine were good friends from church, so she wouldn't have told me anything but the truth. Effie said she'd go and check for me, though. Next thing I know, Mr. Daniel Worthington came down to meet me at the door and he was mad as a wet hen. I'll never forget that scowl of his. He snatched up that package like he already knew what was in it, told me never to come back, and then slammed the door. Effie wouldn't talk about it except to stand by her story that Deanie hadn't come to the Worthington home, though she promised she'd let me know the moment she or that baby showed up. I knew then what had happened. That old man paid her off."

"Why?" Meredith asked. "This was his great-grandchild."

"He didn't think it was. I don't know for sure, but I'm willing to bet Thomas Sr. was behind it all. If Ben had a child, then that meant his line had to share the inheritance with his brother Simon's line, so Thomas probably put that idea in his daddy's head. Or maybe he didn't. Only the Lord knows, since those men are long gone."

"I don't know," Julia said. "That seems rather extreme, especially since he wouldn't live to see that money distributed. Plus he already had plenty."

"There are folks who would say they never have enough no matter how much they have." Maggie Lu shrugged. "Thomas Worthington Sr. was that kind of man."

"But Tommy Two was always so sweet and generous," Meredith said.

"Like his mama," Maggie Lu said. "She was a gem."

"Hold on," Julia said. "Even if Thomas schemed against Simon's line inheriting and Daniel was set on not believing that child was his grandson's, wouldn't Wilhelmina have weighed in on this? From what I've read, she ruled the roost."

"After Daniel died, she ruled the roost, but before then? Oh no." She paused. "It's also possible she had no idea what was going on in her house. Remember, it was a big house and those people rarely spoke to one another. Other than Thomas Sr. and his daddy, who were thick as thieves except for that falling out they had right before the old man died. Only Wilhelmina could tell us, and she's obviously not going to do that."

"No," Julia said slowly, "but maybe the records will speak for her. We just have to keep digging and asking questions."

"All right, ladies," Charlene called as she stepped out of the kitchen carrying two shopping bags. "You're all set."

Maggie Lu leaned forward, her eyes first on Julia and then on Meredith. "Have you talked to Sunny Worthington yet?" Her voice was low, her expression unreadable.

"She's next on our list," Meredith told her.

"Be sure that you do," she said. "Ask her about her rose."

"Rose? Like the flower?" Julia asked. "As in gardening?"

Meredith shook her head. What in the world was she talking about?

Charlene arrived at the table and handed the bags to them then slipped back into the booth beside her mother. A moment later, the conversation veered back to the details of the baby shower. They laughed and planned and sipped iced tea until customers started to filter in for dinner.

"I could stay here all night," Charlene said, "but if I'm not there to supervise, chaos reigns."

"Child, you know that is not true," Maggie Lu told her. "You hire only the best, and you train them to do everything exactly like you want it done."

"Well, that is true." Charlene stood. "Ladies, truly, I am so thankful for all you're doing for Clarissa and the baby. We are blessed."

Julia rose to hug Charlene and Meredith followed suit. "Let us know if you think of anything else we can do," Julia told her. "Just send us an email."

"Be sure and copy Carmen," Meredith said. "That way we won't forget to do it."

"I need a Carmen," Charlene said. "I write myself notes. You should see my office back there. For that matter, you should see the kitchen. No. Actually, you shouldn't. You'd think I've lost my mind."

"Charlene," someone called from the kitchen. "Would you come taste this?"

She made a face. "Sorry, but I have to go. Mama, are you going to stay for the dinner shift? I'll drive you home after I get everyone situated in the kitchen."

"Nonsense," Maggie Lu said. "I'm fine taking the bus."

"I won't hear of it," Julia told her. "I'll drop you off. I've got to run an errand that's not far from your house, Maggie Lu. It'll be no trouble at all."

"Thank you, then. I will take you up on that offer," she said as she followed them out to the parking lot.

Meredith's SUV was parked by Julia's car in the far corner of the lot. The wind had picked up while they were in the diner, and the cold was settling in. She'd have two blankets on the bed again tonight.

Oh how she missed summer. But then, when it was hot she longed for the first signs of fall and cooler temperatures.

Meredith buttoned her jacket and wished for the warm scarf she'd left at the office. Regal as ever, Maggie Lu looked perfectly put together and completely unaffected by the cold.

While Julia loaded her bag of food into the trunk, Meredith waited with Maggie Lu. "Back to what you said about Sunny

Worthington," she urged. "She's going to think I've lost my mind if I ask her to tell me about her rose. Could you elaborate?"

Maggie Lu looked as if she might consider it. Then she shook her head. "That's Sunny's story to tell."

"Okay," Meredith said for lack of any other response. She was still trying to figure out what Maggie Lu meant as Julia drove away.

Shaking her head, Meredith pushed the button that opened the hatch on her SUV then deposited the bag there. After closing the hatch, she stepped back in time to see a movement from the corner of her eye.

A person on a skateboard zipped past on the other side of the street. He wore a helmet, yellow hoodie, and lime-green baggy pants—basically the uniform of a skateboarder—and the likelihood that it was Kenneth "Skate" Worthington was slim to none.

But didn't skateboarders stick together? And if a famous skateboarder was anywhere near Savannah, maybe the word was out among his fellow boarders.

It was worth a try.

Meredith took off in the direction he'd gone and then realized the folly of trying such a feat on foot. She climbed into her SUV and gave chase.

She caught up with the skateboarder at the edge of the small park that was located about a quarter mile from the diner. Though she was aware there was a patch of trees with picnic tables, she hadn't noticed until now that there was a skate park tucked into the back of the space.

She parked, palmed her keys, and set off toward the skate park. As she got nearer, the sound of wheels on concrete competed with the whoops and cheers of what sounded like a few dozen skaters.

When she turned the corner and spied the skate park, she stopped short. Though the skater on the street had been wearing what she thought was distinctive lime-green and yellow clothing, she was stunned to see that the garb was not distinctive at all. In fact, every one of the skaters here had on the same thing.

"Excuse me," she called, acutely aware of how much older she was than these kids. "Could one of you help me?"

"Are you lost, ma'am?"

She turned to see a skater pull off his helmet beside her. No, he was a she—a pretty young woman with silky golden hair tumbling down below her shoulders.

"Oh, well, no," Meredith managed as she tried to contain her surprise. "Actually, I was wondering if any of you know Skate Worthington."

The girl's features went slack. "You're in Savannah at a skate park, and we're a skate team practicing for a competition on Saturday. Of course we know him." Then her eyes narrowed. "Why?"

Several responses came to mind. Meredith decided to go with the one that required the least explaining and no direct untruths. "I saw his sister this morning, and it made me wonder if he was in town too. I need to talk to him about some family stuff. Do you know if he might be?"

The girl laughed and gestured toward the half-dozen yellow posters that had been plastered in a row across the side of the skate ramp. At the top of each one in green letters it said SKATE WITH SKATE! Beneath that headline was a picture of a smiling Skate Worthington followed by a long list of events that would be taking place at the skating competition on Saturday.

At the same time as the shower.

Meredith groaned. "I have my answer," she told the girl. "Thanks."

Her cell phone rang, and she reached into the pocket of her coat to retrieve it. "Julia? Is something wrong?"

"I just dropped off Maggie Lu."

Meredith moved toward the parking lot, the sounds of the skaters echoing behind her.

"Where are you?" Julia demanded.

"A skate park. It's a long story, but I found Kenneth Worthington. He'll be the special guest at a Skate with Skate! event on Saturday."

"Saturday," Julia echoed. "So can we catch up to Skate and still make the shower?"

"Probably not," Meredith said. "The poster said the event starts at the same time as the shower. Also, I don't know that we'll get much conversation out of him when he's the center of attention. We'll have to strategize about this. Hold on a sec. I'm getting in my car."

She clicked her key fob to open the door then climbed inside and shut out the cold. Turning the ignition, she put the phone on hands-free speaker and then turned up the heater.

"Okay, much better. Those kids were out there skating in sweatshirts. Can you imagine?"

Julia chuckled. "Back to Maggie Lu. What do you think?"

"I think when we meet with Sunny, we're going to have to ask her what it all means."

"Should we have Carmen set the appointment with her tomorrow, then?" Julia asked.

"You know, I think maybe I should call her. I was on several committees with her at the historical society, and Chase went to school with her kids." Her phone buzzed. It was Quin. "I need to grab this. I'll let you know when we can go see her."

She signed off and switched in time to catch Quin before he hung up. "I wasn't sure if I'd be able to catch you," he said. "I got your text. Are you serious about dinner?"

"Well, I am currently as full as a tick on a hound dog." Meredith told him about her afternoon at the diner. "However, Charlene said she tucked something into the bag for you to have for dinner, so you're not completely out of luck."

"If it's from Downhome Diner, I'm in."

Meredith chuckled. "Okay then. I'm headed home now. I'll put your dinner in the warming drawer so you can show up whenever it is convenient."

"I'm working on a patent matter right now, but I ought to be able to leave the office in an hour, maybe less."

Meredith caught a flash of yellow in her rearview mirror. The practice must be ending. She returned her attention to Quin.

"That's fine," she told him. "I'll see you then."

Her vehicle's passenger door opened, and a skateboarder flung himself inside. Or perhaps herself. The distinction wasn't immediately apparent. Meredith stifled a scream and then let out a long breath.

"Meredith!" Quin shouted over the speakers of her car. "What's wrong? Are you in danger? Do I need to call 911?"

The stranger removed his helmet to reveal the shaggy blond hair and smiling face of Skate Worthington. Kate's twin retrieved a half-empty bottle of water from the pocket of his hoodie and took a long drink, obviously enjoying both the water and the fact he had caught her by surprise.

"No, I'm fine," she said as Quin continued to express his concern. "I just didn't expect you to do that," she said to Skate.

"Do what? I heard the car door open," Quin insisted. "Who are you talking to?"

"I'm fine," she repeated. "I came to the skate park looking for someone, and I asked if anyone could help me find him. He found me instead."

"And you're sure you're fine?"

"I promise she's fine. I thought she saw me coming or I would have knocked on the window instead of just jumping inside." Kenneth raised his water bottle as if offering a toast. "We wear bright colors for visibility, you know. Skate Worthington, by the way."

"So, you're Kenneth Worthington." Meredith paused to scrutinize the scruffy skater. "Kate's twin."

Skate cringed. "Yeah, unfortunately. I guess I don't look much like the weather girl."

"Actually you look just like her," she said as her gaze took in the high cheekbones, green eyes rimmed with thick lashes, and the upturned nose that looked handsome on him and feminine on Kate. If she had to describe him, she would say he looked like a young Keith Urban.

"I get that," he said.

"Except in height," she amended. "You're much taller."

"I would hope so." He shrugged.

"Meredith, why is Kenneth Worthington in your car?" Quin asked. "I just played tennis with his stepfather this morning."

She spared the intruder a quick glance then looked down at the phone. "I was looking for him regarding a case and thought the skate park might be a good place to start. It was. He found me, and here we are."

"Okay. Do you need more time?" Quin asked.

"No, it won't take long," she said.

"All right. I guess I'll see you in an hour. Or thereabouts."

He quickly hung up, leaving silence to fall between Meredith and her surprise guest. "Thank you for finding me."

He shrugged. "Okay, so what do you want with me?"

She decided to take the direct route to her goal. "A DNA test."

Chapter Eleven

LATER THAT EVENING, WHILE QUIN enjoyed his fried chicken dinner at the island in Meredith's kitchen, she told him all about her conversation with Kenneth Worthington. "So when I explained why I needed the DNA test in order to qualify him as an heir, he seemed interested."

"What thirty-year-old wouldn't want a share of what I imagine is a lot of money?" Quin asked.

"Apparently this one," she said. "I told him Kate was doing it too, and that he needed to call ahead before he went in to have it done. I was about to hand him a card from Theo's law firm when he suddenly bolted and ran like a scared rabbit. It was the oddest thing."

His eyes narrowed. "What could have caused that?"

"I don't know," she told him. "I was parked in a public parking lot on a fairly busy street. Any number of cars passed us, but no one stopped or paid us the least interest. I got out of the car and shouted after him, but he just kept running."

"Do you want me to speak to Chip about persuading him to take the test?"

She shook her head. "Not yet. Skate might have skated, but he left his water bottle behind."

"And his DNA," Quin supplied.

"And his DNA," she echoed. "I'll drop it off with Theo tomorrow and let him work out the legalities and permissions to use it. It's not exactly what was requested as a sample, but hopefully it will serve the purpose. I like having science to back up my work, and this just might do it." Meredith grinned. "Speaking of tests, hurry up and finish your chicken. I'm ready to test these desserts."

Meredith's phone rang. She glanced over at Quin, who had just pulled another chicken leg from the box Charlene packed for him. "It's Julia. Do you mind if I take it?"

"Go ahead," he said. "Take your time. I'm doing just fine here."

"You look like you are," she said with a chuckle before connecting to the call with Julia and offering a greeting.

"I'm so sorry to interrupt your dinner with Quin, but I just got off the phone with my lawyer friend in New York and thought you would want to hear what he discovered about Trey Worthington."

She glanced over her shoulder at her dinner guest. Quin Crowley was a respected attorney and a trustworthy man. However, he was not her client and probably shouldn't hear any part of this conversation, even if it was just her part.

Meredith moved into her study and closed the door. "Okay," she said as she settled on the settee by the window. "What did you find out?"

"It's as we guessed it," Julia said. "Trey was in the witness protection program and is, according to my friend, completely unreachable. If he's still alive, which is something my friend couldn't confirm. The fact that he went into the program is all that could be determined. What happened after that? No one could tell him."

Meredith tried to imagine what it would be like to need a new life so desperately that it was worth leaving everything in your old life behind. Worse, to die alone without old friends or family even aware of it.

It was beyond her ability to even consider that sort of death, much less that sort of life. How lonely Trey must have been. And how afraid.

"That seems hard to believe," she told Julia. "I don't know how those things work, but wouldn't there be someone within the program who would know where he is in case there's some sort of an emergency?"

"Apparently not," she said. "Or if there is, he either doesn't know about it or isn't talking."

"That's too bad."

"Agreed, which is why I made another call. I'm on friendly terms with a state Supreme Court justice in New York. I called only to brainstorm another way of reaching out to Trey or, in the alternative, to see if he's even still alive. He gave me a number to call."

"For Trey?"

"No, for the person handling his case."

"So he's still alive?" Meredith asked.

"I don't know." Julia paused. "We can decide how to go forward on this tomorrow at the office. I just wanted to let you know I made some progress. Now get back to Quin. I've taken you away from him for too long."

Meredith chuckled. "I think he'd complain more if you took him away from Charlene's chicken. The man is happily munching away in my kitchen right now. He told me not only did he not mind me taking this call but that it was fine with him if I took my time."

They shared a laugh. Then silence fell between them.

"I'm glad you're not going through boxes tonight," Julia said. "I think Quin is good for you."

Meredith agreed. "He's a good friend. However, we've already decided we have to make it an early night because we've got work to do. He's in trial next week. So, it looks like I'll be spending part of my evening with the Worthington boxes after all. Just not all of it."

"I'll take that small victory," Julia said. "See you tomorrow."

Meredith hung up and, before she returned to her dinner guest, shot off a quick text to Sunny Worthington asking if she could set aside time to meet regarding a matter related to the Worthington family as soon as possible. If Maggie Lu was adamant that she should ask about a rose, then she would ask about it.

She pressed SEND, telling herself that it was likely that Kate had already told her mother about their visit this morning, and she would be expecting to be contacted. The worst that could happen was that Sunny could ignore her. Then she'd be forced to call.

Meredith went back to the kitchen to find Quin staring at his phone. "Is something wrong?" she asked him.

"Come look at this." He nodded toward the phone in his hand. "I got a breaking news alert and clicked on it. My daughter's friend is the reporter on the scene. I try to watch her reports when I get a chance."

Meredith settled onto the stool beside Quin and looked down at the phone. There was a woman with a WSVG microphone in hand, the red and blue lights of emergency vehicles turning her skin garish colors as she stood on the curb near the diner.

"Turn that up, please," Meredith said.

Quin pressed the button that controlled the volume.

"Witnesses say the car that hit him accelerated just before impact, throwing the victim into the parking lot here at the Downhome Diner. He came to land a few yards from where I am standing, and that's where emergency personnel found him." The reporter looked into the camera with a take-me-seriously-I-am-a-reporter expression. "And that is where the story takes an even stranger turn."

Meredith glanced over at Quin. "What?" she asked. "Who is this victim they're talking about? Is it someone we know?"

"Kenneth Worthington," he said.

"Skate? Is he…?" She couldn't say it.

"Meanwhile, the search is still on not only for the attacker but for the victim as well," the reporter continued.

"Wait." Meredith shook her head. "How did they lose Kenneth? He'd been hit by a car, for goodness' sake. He couldn't just get up and run away, could he?"

Quin shrugged. "One wouldn't think so, but it sounds like he did. I should call Chip."

"Yes, please do that," Meredith said. "I need to text Julia and tell her to turn on the news."

***

The next morning Meredith arrived at the office to find Julia waiting for her. It was too early for Carmen to arrive, but Julia had brought coffee for both Meredith and herself from the Sentient Bean. After Meredith deposited her coat, purse, and a couple of boxes in her office, she headed back down the hall to Julia's office.

"Have they found Kenneth?" Julia asked when she settled on the chair across the desk from her.

"As of an hour ago, no," Meredith told her. "Quin was on the phone to Chip this morning for an update, but there is none. The family is beside themselves, as you can imagine."

"Kate wasn't on the news this morning. I suppose that's to be expected."

Meredith shrugged. "I guess so. I feel bad now that I left a voice mail for Sunny to call me last night regarding the Worthington matter. When I texted her, I had no idea her son was missing."

"After being hit by a car," Julia added. "That is the part I'm really stuck on. It's so odd."

"It is, Julia. Kenneth told me that he wears bright colors for visibility. When I saw him last night, he was wearing a neon-yellow hoodie. All the skaters at the park were."

"So he would be easily seen by a driver," Julia supplied.

"Witnesses said the driver sped up right before impact," Meredith said. "Combine that with high-visibility clothing, and this adds up to someone intentionally trying to hurt him."

"Or just trying to teach a lesson to a skater," Julia said. "Kids on skateboards are not universally loved."

"Well, true." Meredith thought of the times she had grumbled at kids who were riding their boards up and down the rails outside the historical society's headquarters. "I suppose this could be someone who had a grudge against skaters. But even if that explains the hit, it doesn't explain the victim's run," she added. "Why did Kenneth take off?"

"You saw him earlier in the afternoon. Did he do or say anything that might make you think he was afraid of something or someone?"

"Actually," Meredith said, "he did end our conversation rather abruptly. I had just asked him about taking a DNA test when he jumped out of the car and ran. He was in such a hurry to leave that he forgot his water bottle."

"Which I assume you'll deliver to Theo's office so they can run a DNA test on it," Julia said.

"I'll have Carmen drop the water bottle off as soon as she gets here. Now tell me about your conversation last night with—"

The back door opened. "Sounds like she's here," Julia said. "Carmen, is that you?"

"*Sí, señora*," she said and then stepped into view at Julia's door. "You two are here early. Did you hear what happened to Skate Worthington? It's awful."

"Terrible," Julia agreed. "He was just with Meredith a few hours before."

Carmen's mouth opened. "Spill," she said when she recovered her composure. "I love to watch him skate. He's a pro, so I can't believe he didn't manage to avoid that collision. I read that he saw the guy coming and played chicken with him, but I don't believe it. Skaters wouldn't do that. It makes us all look bad. Plus he's a local. Everyone knows Skate Worthington."

"You're a skater, Carmen?"

She lifted one shoulder in a casual shrug. "Sometimes. Not often. I pay too much for these nails to break one doing a frontside flip or an ollie. I go the skate park sometimes but there are too many grommets out there now."

Meredith shook her head. "Carmen, I have no idea what you just said."

"Grommets are little kids who skate. They're cute, but they get in the way and don't always know the rules of skating. I can't really describe a frontside flip or an ollie, but I could show you if I had a board."

"Some other time I would love to see that," Meredith said. "Actually, I've got an errand for you once you've gotten situated. I need you to drop something off at Lucas, Wilson, Kyler & Strong."

Carmen grinned. "Ooh, the cute guy's office?"

"The cute guy's assistant's office," Meredith said. "She'll be expecting you. I sent her an email to let her know you'd be there this morning."

"I'll go ahead and go now," she said. "Anything else while I'm out?"

"No, that's all."

Meredith went to her office and came out with the box labeled WORTHINGTON HEIR #3, the designation they were using for Kenneth Worthington. Inside was a plastic bag containing his water bottle and a note she'd written to Theo with information on how and when the sample was obtained.

"It's a nice morning, so I'll walk." Carmen tucked the box under her arm and headed for the front door. "I need the steps anyway. I'm dreaming of a beach vacation in my not-too-distant future, but I'm absolutely not bikini ready."

"My days of being bikini ready are long gone," Meredith shook her head, laughing, as Carmen opened the front door and stepped outside.

Meredith returned to Julia's office. "Did you hear that?"

Julia looked up from her laptop. "I'm sorry, what?"

"Nothing. Just Carmen being Carmen. Are you okay?"

"Yes, sorry. I'm fine. I was just reading through my notes from my conversations last night about Trey Worthington."

Meredith returned to the seat she'd just vacated. "We were about to get to that when Carmen came in."

"I was given a number to call," Julia said. "But I thought it best to wait until today during business hours."

Meredith sat on the edge of her seat. "Call it!"

Julia picked up her phone and punched in the number, referring to her computer screen midway through. Then she pushed SEND to place the call and waited, pushing the button to activate the speaker function.

After the third ring, a masculine voice said, "Yes?"

"My name is Julia Foley—Judge Julia Foley, retired," she corrected. "I was given your number by Judge Martin Grimes. He accepted a plea deal from a defendant and allowed him to be taken into WITSEC."

"Okay." This time the voice was more hesitant. Deeper.

"Our office is in need of information regarding Mr. Thomas Worthington III for the purposes of a legal matter. I realize this is highly unorthodox and unusual, and I'd be very happy to arrange a face-to-face meeting so my claims could be validated, but we have a need to determine if he is alive and, should he be proven to be alive, we need a DNA sample." She paused a second. "Before you say no or hang up on me, I should tell you that his portion of the inheritance in question is quite a substantial figure."

"And?"

Julia exchanged a glance with Meredith then shook her head. "And we cannot give him his portion until we can qualify him as an heir."

"Tell me who you talked to again."

"Judge Martin Grimes."

The phone went dead.

"Well, all right then," Meredith said. "Someone needs to brush up on his manners."

Julia snatched up her phone. "I'll call him back. Maybe we just got disconnected."

After hitting redial and activating the speaker, Julia set the phone down on the desk between them once again. After two rings, the line went dead. On the next attempt, the same thing happened.

Julia frowned. "I guess he'll call back."

Meredith gave her a look that she hoped would convey how low she believed those odds to be. Then she shrugged. "Okay, well, moving on. I saw nothing new in the news this morning. Just a rehash of the details from last night."

"You should contact the police," Julia said. "You do have something to add, what with the way Kenneth behaved so strangely in your car."

"You're right. I should call." Meredith shook her head. "No, I think I'll go down to the police station. You never know what I'll find out while I'm there."

"Good idea," Julia said. "Meanwhile, I'll wait for a call back from Mr. Chatty."

Chapter Twelve

MEREDITH WALKED INTO THE CENTRAL precinct of the Savannah Police Department and looked around. When she couldn't make heads or tails of which direction to go, she decided to cut a path straight to the front desk and the uniformed officer who watched her approach.

"May I help you, ma'am?"

"I need to speak with someone in regard to the Kenneth Worthington matter." She paused to choose her words carefully, noting that the name on his uniform was Barry Pratt. "I've got some information that the team investigating the incident yesterday might find valuable."

The officer studied her a moment, expression neutral. "Like what? We get a lot of people coming around wanting to be part of something bigger than themselves. So prove to me you're not one of them."

She shifted positions and held on tight to the straps of her purse. "Like I just might be the last person to speak to Kenneth Worthington before he was hit by that car, Officer Pratt."

That got his attention. "Why didn't you say so? Come with me."

He came around the desk to usher her down a hallway. They passed three doors before he opened one, nodding for her to go inside.

The door clanged shut behind her as Meredith took in her surroundings. A metal table slightly smaller than the one in their conference room at Magnolia Investigations sat in the middle of the room beneath a metal pendulum lamp with a cage over the bulb. The walls were painted a pale beige, and the floor was covered in what appeared to be the same linoleum that her doctor's office used in the exam rooms.

Oddly, the table only hosted three chairs, with two on one side and one on the other. Behind the pair of chairs was a mirrored wall.

"Oh," she said out loud as she looked at her reflection in the mirror. "There are people watching me in there, aren't there?" She moved closer. "I'm perfectly normal and sane, I promise, and my information is true."

"I'm glad to hear it, ma'am," a masculine voice said as the door opened. "We prefer the truth around here."

Meredith turned around and froze. Standing in the doorway was Ron's old partner, a former Georgia Tech defensive lineman who treated any obstacle like a Georgia Bulldog quarterback and tackled it head on. That quality, along with the banter that came with supporting rival college football teams, was what had kept Ron and Wally's friendship alive in the decades since Ron left the force.

She hadn't seen Wally since the funeral two years ago, though he'd sent the occasional message of support via email, and his smile brought welcome relief. "Wally?"

"Hello, Meredith."

"Wallace Parker." She grinned and stepped into his embrace. "I thought you retired and moved down to the Keys."

"I did." They parted, and he nodded toward the table. "Hated it. Em and I were going stir-crazy sitting on the porch staring at the water, and there's only so many times a day you can take the boat out or fish. Sometimes paradise is what's familiar and not what everyone else says it is." He shook his head. "Anyway, it's good to see you, young lady. Sit down and tell me why you're here. Something about being a witness?"

"In the Kenneth Worthington matter," she said as she sat with the mirrored wall behind her. "I think I might be able to fill in a little of what happened in the time leading up to the incident with the car."

He retrieved a small leather notebook out of his shirt pocket. Its resemblance to the one Ron used to carry sent a pang of sadness through her heart. *This grief thing…*, she mused as she tucked the memory back where it belonged and offered Wally a smile…*it never fails to surprise me.*

When he was ready to write, Wally nodded. "You know the drill. Start at the beginning."

"Julia and I are working on a case—finding all the heirs to Wilhelmina Worthington's will—and I was looking to meet with Kenneth Worthington to see if I could get a DNA sample from him to qualify him as a legal heir."

One dark brow rose. "You're not sure about him? Chip and Sunny's whole life has been played out in the society columns. I'm pretty sure that his birth, and his sister's, would have been announced like the Second Coming."

Meredith made a note to check the newspaper archives to add any baby announcements to her file. "The stakes are high, so I prefer to have science to back up whatever I put in my report and confirm everyone is who they say they are."

She paused as Wally scribbled notes. At his nod, she continued. "I went looking for Kenneth and found him at the park just down the street from the Downhome Diner. Or, rather, he found me."

"How did that happen?" Wally asked.

"I saw skaters and thought maybe someone there could tell me how I might locate him." She went on to explain the series of events that led to Kenneth climbing into her SUV. "I was talking to Quin on speaker phone—that's Quin Crowley. He's an attorney in town and is a friend of mine. He heard most of the conversation."

"So he would be willing to corroborate your testimony of the events."

"He would." She gave him Quin's phone number then continued with her story. "In the middle of our conversation about the DNA test, Kenneth just bolted and ran from my vehicle without a word of explanation or a backward glance, leaving his water bottle behind."

"Which you will likely have tested for DNA," he said with a half smile.

"Exactly." She paused. "Or rather, the legal firm in charge of the estate's distribution will. But the point is, we were having a perfectly calm and rational conversation and then he just took off. It was the oddest thing."

"And there was nothing that appeared to set him off? No one walking by or a vehicle he took notice of?"

"Nothing like that," she said. "Although there were plenty of cars on the street at that time of day, so he may have seen something I missed."

"Which direction did he go?"

"North," she replied. "I called after him but didn't consider following since he was on his skateboard. I could never have caught up to him."

"Okay. Once he disappeared did you try to call him?"

"No. His sister, Kate, had given me his phone number, but I didn't think to use it at the time. Do you need it?"

"Go ahead and give it to me. I'll add it to our information."

She gave him the number and then put her phone away. "Are there any leads on whoever aimed a car at Kenneth?"

Wally put his pen down and met Meredith's gaze. "Not yet. Except for the sudden acceleration just before impact, this appears to be a random hit-and-run." He paused. "Until you get to the part where the victim does the running, that is. And no, we haven't found any trace of him. At this point, we're looking for him with hopes he turns up at a hospital or clinic—awful as that sounds."

"No, I understand. If he's hurt, he needs to get help. And if he's afraid to get help…"

"Exactly." Wally folded his hands together. "Did he mention any threats against him or indicate in any way that he was frightened of someone?"

She thought back over the conversation then shook her head. "No, nothing like that. Unless I'm forgetting something. It was just a perfectly normal conversation where he introduced himself and I marveled at how he looked like a young Keith Urban. Silently, I mean," she hastened to add. "Telling him that on our first meeting would have been weird."

Wally scribbled something then looked up at her again. "This case you're working on, could it be related to the incident?"

Meredith paused to consider the question. "All named heirs are to share in the proceeds of a trust that is substantial. We've got three individuals who we're pretty sure of and one more we may be able to verify once the DNA tests come back. If there are four heirs, each stand to get somewhere in the neighborhood of $25 million."

He whistled. "That's a nice neighborhood. And also a possible motive for taking out a fellow heir. Other than the Worthington twins and possibly Trey Worthington, who else are you looking at?"

"As heir?" At his nod, she continued. "A woman formerly named Amy Calloway, renamed per a petition to the court as Willadeane Worthington."

"She's local?"

Meredith nodded. "She runs a hospice home for elderly women. We only recently interviewed her, but if you need it, I can give you whatever information you want." She took a breath. "But I can tell you that she seems very nice and normal. Not the kind to run over a skateboarder in broad daylight."

"I'm sure you're right." His pen was poised over the notebook again. "Tell me whatever else you know about her. Contact information would be helpful too."

She blinked. Twice. So he did consider Willadeane a possible suspect. Logically, she understood, but after meeting the woman, it was hard to reconcile.

"I have all of that at the office. How would you like me to get it to you?"

He pulled out a business card and set it on the table in front of her. "Just email it. That'll be fine. And that way I don't have to try and read my own handwriting."

"I'll do that as soon as I get back to the office." She leaned back in her chair, her thoughts swirling. "What have I gotten myself into, Wally? This was supposed to be a simple heir search. Well, maybe not simple given the scale of the investigation and the amount of money involved, but definitely not something I thought would lead to all this."

"Have you ever done a probate or heir search case before?"

"Sure," she said. "We've done a few. Pretty basic stuff. Just find a few folks who might not know they're entitled to something and report back to the client when we've got them all located. Ron did them all the time too. That's where I learned that science bests anything else in the courtroom if your work is challenged."

"If you learned from Ron Bellefontaine, then you know that the almighty dollar is the greatest motivator of all. Jealousy is its close second. And if you are jealous of someone else's money?" He shrugged. "Well, you see what I'm saying."

She did. Hadn't Willadeane gone to great lengths to become a Worthington—to have what they had—first the name change and then claiming a cut of the trust fund?

"Is there anything else you can add to this, Meredith?"

She reined in her racing thoughts to focus on the question. "Just that when I spoke to Kenneth's sister, she expressed some concern over him. I can't put my finger on it, but my instincts said there was more there than an overachieving sister complaining about a brother who preferred to skateboard his way through life."

"You've got an investigator's instinct," Wally said.

"Thanks to Ron," Meredith admitted. "I learned from the best. No offense to you, of course."

He grinned. "None taken. So how are the boys?"

Fifteen minutes later, they'd caught up on their respective families and exchanged photographs of grandchildren. "I've taken up too much of your time," Meredith exclaimed. "I'll send you that information on Willadeane Worthington when I get back to my desk."

"Thank you. I'll walk you out."

They got all the way to the front door of the precinct building before Wally stopped to face her. "One more thing. Do you have any idea what this Willadeane woman drives?"

"I can find out," she said. "Do you have a make on the vehicle involved in the incident?"

Wally appeared to consider his answer before speaking. "We do, based on witness descriptions, and we're hoping to get security camera feed to back up what we've been told. This was in an all-commercial location with no residential areas in view." He shrugged. "Where are all those doorbells with cameras when you need them?"

Meredith chuckled. "Isn't that the truth? I could offer the inventor of those things a big fat kiss for coming up with them. They've factored in on more than one of our successful cases."

"Ours too. Well, you take care, Meredith," Wally said. "It's good to see you again. Maybe you can spare some time to have dinner with Em and me." He paused. "Like the old times."

She matched his smile. "I would like that very much."

They embraced again, and then he opened the door for her to leave. Meredith got all the way to her SUV before she realized that

Wally hadn't fully answered her question about the make of the hit-and-run vehicle.

Turning around, she spied Wally still watching her from the door. Lifting a hand to wave, she muttered under her breath. "Oh, you're good, Wally Parker. But then, you learned from the best too."

Chapter Thirteen

MEREDITH'S PHONE LIT UP WITH an incoming call as she was exiting the parking lot. She activated the call, which originated from an undisclosed number. She made a mental note to turn the ringer back on.

"It's Sunny," the caller said.

"Sunny Worthington?" The name came out on a rush of breath. "Oh, Sunny, I'm so sorry I sent that text last night. I had no idea about Kenneth at the time."

"Can you come over to the river house on Shore Road?"

Her tone was tight, her words clipped as she gave the address for the property. Neither would raise an eyebrow in their social circles. Meredith wondered, however, if concern over her son had her speaking in such a way.

Worrying about a male child was something she understood quite well.

Shore Road was a bit of a drive. Nowhere near where she was now. But she wouldn't miss an opportunity to speak to Sunny Conrad.

"Of course," she said. "Name the time. My schedule is flexible today."

There was a pause and then Sunny said, "Now. If you can."

"I'm on my way."

Thirty minutes later Meredith arrived at the gates to the Conrad home south of downtown near Georgetown on the Little Ogeechee River. The home—an estate, really—was a sprawling gray and white craftsman mansion nestled on a massive wooded property that afforded Chip a tennis court and a dock for the sailboats he loved. This she'd learned from Quin, who made the drive out to play tennis regularly but drew the line at Chip's grand plan for them to sail to Bermuda together.

Unlike their elegant Georgian home adjacent to Forsyth Park where they had raised the twins, this place had all the markings of a casual vacation home. That is, if your budget to purchase and furnish your casual vacation home was in seven figures.

Before she could hit the buzzer, the gates quietly swung open, revealing a broad concrete drive that looked like the perfect spot to land their private jet. Just before the runway met the house, it split off into a roundabout with a grassy center filled with well-behaved tropical plants that surely would be dug up and hurried off to a greenhouse before the first frost.

Meredith parked on the circular drive nearest the house and stepped out in time to see the black lacquered front door open. Sunny stepped onto the wide front porch in what amounted to a very elegant set of pale pink pajamas. More surprising, her always perfectly coiffed blond hair had been tamed into a messy ponytail and it appeared she was not wearing even a hint of makeup.

The Worthington pearls, however, still marched in a single perfect eight-millimeter line around Sunny's neck, with two more pearls mounted as solitaires in her earlobes. Eight millimeters being the perfect size, according to Mama, who cast herself as the arbiter of all things Savannah society.

"Seven is far too dainty for a grown woman, and nine shows you're trying too hard. Anything above that is just plain tacky unless you're going to a costume party dressed as Wilma Flintstone or Betty Rubble."

Meredith cast another glance at Sunny and smiled. Apparently all decorum had not been thrown to the winds with her escape from Savannah.

"Come in quickly," Sunny demanded. "Chip thinks there are drones flying around the house in town trying to catch a glimpse of us for the papers. I think he's been hit by a tennis ball one too many times, but we have been inundated with calls from the press, so he doesn't want us taking any chances. That's why I fled out here."

"Drones?" Meredith glanced behind her then looked overhead. The skies were a clear blue that only early November seemed to provide. "I don't see any."

"According to Chip, they're fast."

"Yes, of course."

Sunny stepped back to allow Meredith to step into a wide foyer paneled with gleaming white wood and, much like the runway outside, a straight shot toward the back of the building and out into a lawn that ended at the river. On either side were glimpses of rooms decorated in creamy whites and lit by the lamps of glittering crystal chandeliers.

Her hostess veered to the left abruptly, and Meredith almost missed the turn for gaping at the pale gray rock fireplace that spanned more than two stories in height and easily fifteen feet in length. An ornately carved gold-framed mirror set above the mantel sparkled with the reflection of a chandelier that was larger than her SUV.

On one end of the room, sunlight shone through floor-to-ceiling windows that overlooked a broad deck and, beyond that, the river. A pair of french doors had been propped open to allow a rather chilly breeze to waft in.

On the other end, Sunny was pouring coffee from a gleaming chrome machine that would make a Starbucks barista green with envy. The middle portion of the kitchen—the part that contained the actual means of preparing and storing food, such as a stove and a bank of glass-front refrigerators with perfectly aligned contents—looked as if no one had ever used anything situated there.

Sunny grabbed both mugs and padded barefoot toward the doors leading to the deck. "Grab that tray, would you?" she tossed over her shoulder as she disappeared outside.

The only tray in sight that didn't appear to be artfully decorated with some form of nautical decor was a silver platter piled with packets of sweetener around an alabaster bowl containing an assortment of individually packaged creamers. A small cut-crystal vase filled with silver spoons sat inside the bowl. It was artful and odd all at the same time. Likely the product of an overzealous cook or housemaid who liked symmetry.

Meredith balanced the tray, which turned out to be heavier than it looked, as she traced Sunny's footsteps outside. She found her hostess seated in a wicker chair beside a rock fireplace that was much more subdued in size and design than the one inside.

After placing the tray on the glass-topped table, Meredith took a seat on a matching wicker chair. Adjusting the blue and white pin-striped cushions to suit her, she waited for Sunny to say or do something.

Finally the silence stretched too long between them. "Aren't you worried about drones?" Meredith asked her.

"Of course not," Sunny said. "I only came here to appease him."

Meredith reached for her mug and grinned. "I doubt he appreciated the remark about being hit in the head with a tennis ball."

Sunny grinned, but her smile didn't last. She looked away, turning her attention toward the river. "Thank you for coming all the way out here."

"Thank you for speaking with me," Meredith countered. "Though I feel like I need to ask you how I can help rather than grill you with the questions I had prepared."

Shifting positions, Meredith reached for her coffee, past the plethora of blooming white cymbidium orchids in blue and white pots. Only then did she notice that the ceramic mug was emblazoned with letters that spelled out So what? Nobody wants to hear it. Meredith turned her mug around to see matching letters with a different statement: Why are you still talking?

"Cute," she said when she caught Sunny watching her.

"Officially they're not mine, but I like them. They were a Christmas gift to Kate from her brother. She didn't see the humor in them." She paused. "But then, she rarely does anymore. Not when it comes from her brother."

"Sunny," Meredith said, seizing the opportunity to steer the topic toward the reason she'd come, "do you know where he is?"

"Probably," she said with a sigh. "My son is fairly predictable. Although I will admit I never saw this coming. He and Kate may be twins, but they're so very different."

Meredith's first question might have come from the mind of an investigator, but the next question came from a mother's heart. "Is he okay?"

Sunny met her gaze. "I hope so."

Meredith sat back. Neither question had been answered as expected. She decided to try a more direct route. "What happened to him yesterday and why?"

"Do you want to know what I know or what I think?"

"Both. Either. I'm so worried about Kenneth. I was there when he first ran off, and I'm still baffled by his behavior. Something spooked him. The change in his demeanor was instantaneous. That he got hit by a car not long after is not a coincidence."

"No," she said slowly as she took another sip of coffee. "It wasn't."

Meredith elected to wait her out, prolonging the time by reaching over to retrieve a silver spoon and a hazelnut creamer. "What do you want to tell me, Sunny?" she finally asked.

"Kenneth is in trouble," Sunny said, cupping the mug in perfectly manicured hands. "He's never been forthcoming with the details of his life, much less so since Kate became so successful and thrust him into the spotlight."

"He has his own spotlight," Meredith argued. "When I asked the kids at the skate park about him, they all knew who he was. There were posters advertising an event that would allow them to 'skate with Skate.'"

"Kate hates that name."

Meredith shook her head. "I don't see how Kate gets a vote."

Sunny smiled. "So we agree on that." She paused and shifted positions, turning toward the fire. "I've always encouraged the children to be individuals. And Chip has always treated the twins as his very own, willing to spend what it took to help them make their dreams come true. The emphasis here is on helping them, because in order to achieve our help, they had to take action. Though it may look that way on the outside, things were not just given to Kenneth and Kate."

Meredith thought of the awards on Kate's wall. Of her popularity as the morning weather anchor and the way she exuded confidence and poise. And in his own way, Kenneth was, as Carmen told her, a pro. He'd reached the top of the heap in the skateboarding world.

"I'm afraid we've instilled a little too much autonomy in our children. They've each grown into the independent adults we hoped they'd become, but Kate views her brother as totally lacking in any self-motivation or drive and considers him lazy. She's never approved of her brother's chosen path—to the extent that they are now no longer on speaking terms. That's just…" Her voice wavered, and she let out a long breath. "Well," she said with renewed vigor, "it's unacceptable."

"Sunny," Meredith said gently, "what does any of this have to do with the emergency that surrounds your son?"

"He's hiding, Meredith," she said, acid now in her tone. "And the person who hit him with that car wants him dead."

"Who? And why?" she blurted out.

"He won't tell us. Chip has tried to get him to talk. Right after it happened, Kenneth called Chip to let him know he was all right."

She mustered a smile. "Apparently, one of the skills a skateboarder learns is how to fall and not get hurt. He told Chip that the vehicle only grazed him, which is why he could get right back up and run after he regained his senses."

"But why did he run? First responders were on the scene."

"Thank the Lord for free meals for emergency personnel at the Downhome Diner. If not for that, there might not have been two EMTs right there when it happened. The pair immediately went to Kenny to perform triage. They told us they were able to tell that his injuries weren't severe, but before they could treat him, as you know, he bolted."

"Just like he did when he was in my SUV," Meredith added. "Have the police indicated who they think might be a suspect?"

"No."

"My personal concern is that someone doesn't want him alive to inherit his portion of his great-grandmother's estate," Meredith said. "You mentioned Kenneth was predictable. So, where would he likely have gone?" Meredith did not look away as she continued. "I'm afraid the person who did this will try again. Kenneth needs to be in protective custody." She glanced around and then returned her attention to her hostess. "Or at least somewhere safe with you and Chip."

"When I married Spencer, I married into the upper tier of Savannah society. My former mother-in-law was presented as a debutante at the Christmas Cotillion. There, she met her future husband, Thomas Sr.—he was escorting another debutante 'of a lesser quality,' as he always put it—and married him before a year was out then joined the Junior League. Under Grandmother Wilhelmina's tutelage, they raised both of their sons to believe it was their responsibility to carry on the family name and social ranking with dignity, understanding that they would always be in the Savannah spotlight."

Meredith was about to ask what any of that had to do with Kenneth when Sunny continued.

"Since Spencer's death, I've rejected the idea that my children should live their lives in fear of the scrutiny of high society. I want them to be true to their own selves, whatever they determine that to be." She shrugged. "But Kate seems to have inherited the Worthington's high expectations and the drive to keep up appearances. As a result, Kenneth and Kate aren't on speaking terms. Her brother is an embarrassment to her."

Meredith placed her cup on the table in front of her and sat back. Enough was enough. No more stalling.

"Sunny Conrad, you've skated around the answers to my questions too long...."

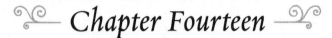

Chapter Fourteen

MEREDITH REALIZED WHAT SHE'D JUST said and froze. This was an awful time to make a skater joke, even an unintentional one. The absolute worst time ever.

A heartbeat later, it dawned on Sunny, and she began to giggle. Of course, Meredith joined her.

"Oh, Meredith," Sunny managed after a few minutes of laughter. "I needed that. Thank you." Then she sobered. "Kenneth has gotten himself into trouble with someone. I think he owes money. Chip believes it could be something else. Whatever it is, I think my son traded good sense for his current situation, and he did it to show Kate that he wasn't the slacker she claims he is."

"Forgive me for stating the obvious, but if it's money he owes, then couldn't you and Chip help temporarily until Kenneth can pay you back?"

This time Sunny's chuckle held no humor. "Believe me, we would if he would just tell us where to send the money. I threatened to put something out on social media stating, 'To Whom It May Concern: if my son owes you money we will pay you back. Let's talk.' Or something like that."

You'd bring kooks out of the woodwork if you did that, Meredith thought, although she fought to keep her expression neutral.

"Kenneth was apoplectic at the mention of it," she said. "Not that I would really do it. However, that's how I feel. I want to fix this. To bail him out. But he won't let me. He won't let either of us. The thing is, I don't see how he got in so deep. Kenneth never has required much, and he's always taken care of himself."

"I'm sorry." Meredith let out a long breath. "Could he have wagered something against the money he's going to receive from his great-grandmother? Maybe in order to pay for some project he had in the works? I'm grasping at straws here."

"He could have," Sunny said slowly. "Chip told me you were working on the list of heirs. I guess he spoke with Theo recently. He said you and Julia Foley had been hired to verify everyone."

"We have."

"Well, that must be interesting work. I'm sure you'll have plenty of applicants to sift through. I know the crazies started coming around when Wilhelmina died. Her attorney, Theo Sr., did a wonderful job of handling them. But then, from what I understand, he also did a wonderful job of handling Wilhelmina when she was alive, so he's a man up to the task. I hope his grandson can fill his shoes adequately."

"So far I think he has." Meredith paused. "What was she like—Wilhelmina?"

"Terrifying, according to many," Sunny said. "And kind and wonderful, all of these things rolled up into one never-to-be-duplicated person who loved her grandsons, Spencer and Tommy Two, fiercely."

"Oh," Meredith said for lack of any better response. A woman who cut her grandchildren out of her will did not seem like the type who would be remembered so fondly.

"She had four closets full of clothing, one for each season. There wasn't a thing in any of them that didn't have a designer label on it. Chanel was her favorite, but she had plenty of de la Rentas and Diors. Every dress had a matching bag and shoes, and most had scarves for her to wear while she drove that white Eldorado around town. From the pictures I saw of her in her prime, she loved to dress like Jacqueline Kennedy with those pillbox hats and oversized sunglasses. Oh, she was the epitome of elegance." Sunny paused. "These are her pearls."

"Did Spencer tell you anything about his grandfather?"

Sunny's expression softened. "Not much. Spencer was thirteen when Daniel died, but he never had much interaction with him. It was his grandmother he spent the most time with." She paused. "She didn't kill her husband, you know, and neither did Spencer's father. There were rumors, but they weren't true."

"How do you know that?"

"Because Spencer was in the house the night his grandfather died. He told me he heard his grandmother and his father arguing after the funeral home took Daniel away." She paused as if remembering, then a faint smile rose. "He told her she shouldn't have punched the coroner."

"I knew it," Meredith said. "My money was on her all the time."

Sunny shrugged. "As I said, the family matriarch was fierce when it came to protecting her own. Spencer said that her response was that her husband might be a—well, there were some strong words here—but that Daniel was her husband, and she wasn't going to let him have an undignified end to a story that probably ought to have had a less wandering path." She paused a moment and then continued. "Those were supposedly her exact words. 'A less wandering path.' Spencer said he used to wonder, as a child, what that meant. Anyway, thank you for listening to my concerns about Kenneth. I'd better let you get back to Savannah. I'm sure you've got plenty of work to do. Speaking of work, will you be wrapping up the heir search anytime soon?"

"These things take time," Meredith said. "But don't worry. I'm not seeing anything at this point that would prevent Kate and Kenneth from inheriting."

"That's good." Sunny rose. "I'll walk you out."

Meredith followed in silence as they retraced their steps down the long hallway and out onto the porch. "Watch out for drones," Sunny said lightly. "And thank you for coming. I'll call you if I have any news. I promise."

"As will I," Meredith said as she walked across the porch and down the steps toward her SUV. Then she recalled she'd forgotten to ask an important question. "Sunny," she said just before Sunny closed the door, "one more question."

Her hostess popped her head back outside, one hand gripping the doorframe. "Sure. What's up?"

"Does the word *rose* mean anything to you in regard to the Worthingtons?"

"Who told you to ask me that?" she hissed, her voice low and her hand now solidly over the fancy camera doorbell.

Considering the vehemence with which Sunny responded to the question, Meredith elected not to spill the beans on where she'd heard it. "It was during the course of my investigation of the Worthington heirs, so I'm not at liberty say. All I was told is that this is your story to tell."

Sunny closed the distance between them, then she led Meredith to the other side of the SUV, putting the vehicle between her and the camera on her doorbell. "Whoever said that was wrong," she said. "It's Trey's story to tell, not mine."

"Trey isn't here," Meredith reminded her.

"Yes, okay. You're right," she said. "I've kept this secret too long. I don't think I'll see Trey again this side of heaven. Before he died, Tommy told me to give up on trying to find him. That he knew with complete certainty that wherever Trey was, he was doing just fine."

Meredith pursed her lips. She'd had the same hope for him, but she would never say she was certain of it. Had Tommy Two learned where his son had been taken?

Sunny glanced up at the sky, and Meredith wondered if she might be scanning for drones. Then Sunny returned her gaze to her. "Trey was hiding a secret, and I helped him."

"With the Mob?" Meredith blurted out.

"Of course not," she said. "This matter was a little more close to home. A family matter, as it were."

"Worthington family?"

"Yes." Sunny paused. "It didn't help that Katherine was going through her first bout of cancer and Tommy was beside himself trying to look after his wife and the family business. Without any sort of supervision, Trey just…" She seemed at a loss for words.

"Went wild?"

"Exactly, but not in the way you would think. No drugs, and though there was alcohol, I'm sure, he never got in trouble for it. He just took off." She shook her head. "He disappeared. Just like Kenneth has. I had just had a bad miscarriage, and I needed Spencer

24/7, so Trey couldn't count on either his uncle or me being there for him. We didn't know it at the time, but he interpreted our absence from his life as everyone in his family letting him down. So at the age of eighteen, he went out and found a substitute."

"What kind of substitute?" Meredith prompted.

"A wife."

The breath went out of Meredith, and then after a moment, she collected herself. "Trey got married?"

"Briefly, yes." She shook her head. "His father fixed it, of course. Paid for their divorce and made sufficient payment to the bride and her family to make it—and her—go away."

Meredith managed a breathy, "I see."

Nothing in what Sunny just said reconciled with the man she'd known Trey to be. But then, she hadn't expected him to have to go into witness protection after wrangling with the Mob either.

"What does any of this have to do with a rose? Sorry, the information I received was vague."

Sunny's perfectly groomed brows gathered, and she shook her head. "Meredith," she said slowly, "I'm not at liberty to say. And that's all I'm going to say about the matter."

***

Meredith returned to Magnolia Investigations to find Carmen talking to someone on the phone and Julia nowhere to be seen. She walked into her office and deposited her purse on the chair then retrieved her phone and put it on her desk.

Sunny had given her plenty to think about but nothing new to go on. She'd seemed certain Kenneth was fine, and she'd admitted that Chip spoke to him. Maybe Chip said something to Quin that might help.

She reached for her cell to phone Quin. "Unless you're dialing the police, do not make that call."

Meredith looked up to see Carmen standing in the doorway. "Why?"

"You were supposed to email a detective at the Central Division. He got worried when you didn't contact him."

"Oh right." She shook her head. "I was supposed to send Wally the information we talked about."

"Yes, I guess so," Carmen said. "Then I got worried because the police were looking for you, and I didn't know where you were. I started calling people."

"And?"

"And Quin got worried when he couldn't reach you either. Julia didn't know where you were. She said you hadn't told her where you were going other than the police station."

"That's strange. I had my phone with me the whole time." She groaned as she unlocked her phone and found that she had missed texts and calls. "Inside my purse." She groaned again. "In silent mode because I was at a meeting with Wally."

Carmen stood silently in the door, her expression oddly sober. "I was really worried about you," she said. "First Skate Worthington gets hit by a car and disappears, and then you were gone and no one could find you. Detective Parker seemed pretty upset, which made me upset, and then when I called Quin…" She shook her head. "You get the idea."

"I do," Meredith said. "And I'm terribly sorry for worrying everyone. Would you mind calling Detective Parker and Quin and letting them know I'm fine and at the office now? Tell Quin I'll call him in just a bit, but I need to speak with Julia first. I got a call while I was leaving the police department, and I drove out to meet with someone who had information on the case."

Meredith didn't say who. There was no need for Carmen to know she'd met with Sunny Worthington. At least not now.

Carmen turned to leave but Meredith called her back. "Thank you. You handled everything exactly right. And, Carmen, please forgive me for worrying you."

Meredith turned back to her phone, swiping away the notices for all the calls and texts she would have to return later. Julia picked up on the first ring.

Before Julia could say anything, Meredith spoke first. "I know. I scared everyone by dropping off the face of the earth for a while, but I'm back and at my desk, and I promise everything is fine."

"Well, all right," Julia said. "Carmen was frantic. She said the police were looking for you."

"Detective Wally Parker was looking for me. I met with him to let him know what happened at the skate park. When I left I told him I was going straight back to the office, and I promised him I would email him some information about Willadeane Worthington. That didn't happen."

"What *did* happen?"

"Sunny called." She gave Julia an abbreviated version of the events that occurred once she left the police station parking lot. "I'll tell you the rest when I see you. Now I'm back here apologizing to everyone so I can get back to work without having the police put out an all-points bulletin on my SUV or storm the building."

"You are loved, my friend. Appreciate that we care if something happens to you."

"I do," she said. "And I am blessed to be so loved."

"Also," Julia said in that voice she used when she wasn't thrilled to have to say something, "have you considered that whoever was after Kenneth may have seen him with you and will come after you next?"

"No," Meredith said, "but I am thinking about it now."

"I can promise you the police have considered it. Carmen told me so."

Meredith sighed. "Are you coming back to the office today?"

"I'll be there in an hour or so," Julia said. "So make sure you're ready to give me all the details."

Meredith said goodbye and then hurriedly phoned Quin. "I'm fine," she said. "And I'm so sorry."

"I know," he told her. "Carmen told me she called me before the police. Your phone was on silent in your purse. Chip told me you were out at the river house with Sunny. I spoke to him briefly about a business matter and he mentioned it."

Of course. He saw them on the doorbell camera. "She called and asked me to come out. I felt like I needed to do that."

"It was nice of you," he said. "So, is everything else okay?"

"Yes, fine. I just have a lot of work to do."

"I'll let you get started on it," he said, "but please don't take any unnecessary risks until whoever ran into Kenneth Worthington is caught."

She smiled to hear the concern in his voice. "I'll be safe, I promise."

With that, she extracted a reluctant goodbye from Quin then set the phone aside. A few minutes later, she retrieved the file on Willadeane Worthington and placed it on the desk.

She took a photograph of the page where Willadeane listed her contact information and emailed it to Wally with a message apologizing for the delay. Then she went hunting for an answer to the question regarding the vehicle Willadeane drove.

When she had exhausted the file's information, Meredith went to her computer and did a search on the paid data site she used to look up automobile titles. There she found two vehicles registered to Willadeane Worthington, a three-year-old silver passenger van and a 1971 white Cadillac Eldorado convertible.

Interesting.

Meredith hit PRINT on her findings and then went in search of the details of Kenneth Worthington's accident. She found the initial story on the *Savannah Morning News's* online site. At the top of the page, there was an update:

Sources within the Savannah PD confirm that security footage from a nearby business taken at the time of the incident showed the vehicle they are looking for is a classic model white Cadillac Eldorado convertible. There is possible front-end damage in relation to the incident.

Chapter Fifteen

MEREDITH PICKED UP HER PHONE and called Wally Parker. He picked up on the second ring. "I got the message, Meredith," he said, "but I'm glad you made the call too."

"I've got more information," she said. "Willadeane Worthington owns a 1971 Cadillac Eldorado convertible."

"Who are you talking to about me?"

Meredith froze and turned toward the doorway, where a familiar figure stood. "Hello, Willadeane," she said casually, the phone still against her ear. "I was just answering some questions that came up in regard to the Worthington case."

"Willadeane Worthington is there?" Wally asked.

Willadeane frowned. "Why does it matter what I drive?"

"Meredith, is she in the room with you right now?"

"Excuse me just a second," she told Willadeane. "Let me just end this call." Silently, she focused on how to answer Wally. "Yes," she said, her attention on her visitor, "yes, that's it."

"Someone is in route right now. Keep her talking."

"All right. Thank you."

She set the phone down out of Willadeane's sight but didn't end the call. Instead, she pressed the button to activate the speaker.

"Okay, Willadeane, how can I help you?"

Willadeane's expression softened only slightly. "Actually, I was just in the neighborhood running errands before I head out of town for the weekend. My aides gave me a Boss's Day weekend at a spa last year, and I never found time to use it. This year they conspired against me to make me go, so what could I say? Anyway, I thought I would stop by to bring your assistant some cookies. She was so helpful to me when I was here last. I just wanted to say thank you to her, but she isn't at her desk."

"Oh? Well, that's strange." Meredith looked past Willadeane to the hallway then back at her surprise guest. "I'm sure she just stepped out for a minute. I can take them for her."

Willadeane shook her head. "Why were you telling someone what car I drove? And how did you know?"

Time to be honest, at least in part. "I did a background check on you and was confirming details. It's standard for all possible heirs who get past the first hurdle." She paused to offer a smile. "Which you have."

"I have?" Her eyes lit up. "That's great news. Did you get the DNA test?"

"No, but I expect it to come back on Monday. According to Theo, the lawyer representing the estate, the lab only takes two to three business days to complete the test."

Willadeane sagged against the doorframe with the bag of cookies—if that's indeed what she was carrying—in her hand. "That's the best news I've heard in a very long time." She set her bag on the table just inside the office and hurried toward Meredith to envelop her in a hug.

"I cannot wait to tell the ladies—not that most of them will understand, bless them. This is just such good news! Thank you so much, Meredith. And please thank Julia too."

With that, she turned around and raced down the hallway and out the back door. Meredith rose and hurried after her.

"Willadeane, wait!" she called, but the door slammed, and she was gone.

Meredith ran to the door and then thought better of it. She didn't have her phone, and she certainly had nothing to protect herself with should Willadeane come running back inside.

So she locked the door then raced to the front door and locked it too. Then she ran back into her office to snatch up her phone.

"Wally, are you still there?"

"I'm here," he said. "What happened?"

"She's gone! I tried to keep her here, but she left the cookies she brought for Carmen and ran off. She said something about her staff sending her to a spa for the weekend."

"What did I miss?" Carmen asked. "And why is the back door locked? I had to use my key to get in. I just made a very quick run to the post office, and you were still here."

Meredith turned toward her. "Willadeane Worthington was just here. She said she wanted to thank you with cookies for the help you gave her."

Carmen snatched up the bag. "Sweet, that's so kind of her. She's a really nice lady. You know she takes care of old people who don't have families, and she keeps them in her home until they die."

"Don't eat those cookies!" Wally shouted over the phone's speaker.

Carmen dropped the bag and it burst open, sending cookies all over Meredith's new rug. "Who was that, and where did he come from?"

"Savannah PD," came a voice at the front door. "Open up."

"And on the phone," Wally said. "Put the cookies down and answer the door."

Carmen's eyes widened. "Meredith, what's going on here? You told me you didn't do anything that the police would need to be concerned about."

"Go and let the officers in," she said. "It's a long story."

A police officer appeared at Meredith's window and motioned for someone to open the door. Another officer stood behind him, one hand on his gun's holster.

"Ma'am, this is Detective Parker of the Savannah PD," Wally said. "Let my officers in. We're not here to take your boss away."

"I'll do it," Meredith said. "Wally, hang tight while I go unlock the front door."

Meredith opened the door, and the two officers identified themselves as they spilled inside. "Wally Parker is on speaker in my office," she told them. "And the woman who was here went out the back door. I locked it behind her and haven't seen her since."

"Go on and give chase," Wally shouted. "I'll keep tabs on Mrs. Bellefontaine and her assistant."

The back door opened, and a second later someone cried out. Meredith raced past Carmen to see Julia standing on the back steps, her entry blocked.

"Let her in, officers," Meredith shouted. "That's my partner, Julia Foley. Judge Julia Foley."

"Sorry, Judge Foley," one of the officers said. "I didn't recognize you."

Meredith looked down at the steps where fruits and vegetables mingled with cans of chicken soup and a carton of hazelnut creamer. In the midst of the mess, Julia's purse lay half-open with the contents spilling out.

"No problem, officers." Julia lowered her hands slowly. "May I pick up my purse and groceries now?"

"I'll help her," Meredith said. "Go. I don't know which way she went, but she's either in a silver panel van or a '71 Eldorado convertible. You might check at her address. Wally has it. Her care center staff may know where she's headed."

Once the police had vacated the porch, Meredith knelt down to help Julia collect her things. "What in the world just happened, Meredith? You told me you spoke to the police, and they weren't going to storm the building."

"Yes, that's true, but—"

"What did you tell them, for goodness' sake?" Julia interrupted. "Because apparently they didn't like it."

Meredith put the last of the errant cherry tomatoes in the grocery bag and stood. "Come inside," she said wearily as she set the bag on the kitchen counter. "I'll tell you all about it."

"It's a good story, Julia," Carmen said, hurrying ahead of them. "Although I'm a little fuzzy on some of the details."

"Meredith!" Wally's voice echoed toward them down the hall. "Are you still there and are you okay? Someone answer me."

"Who is that?" Julia demanded.

"Wally Parker," Meredith said.

"The detective?" Julia closed the back door and, at Meredith's insistence, turned the lock again.

"Meredith!" Wally shouted.

"Okay, Wally," Meredith called, walking into her office. "I'm fine," she snapped. Then, tempering her voice, she continued. "Thank you for worrying about me. Have your officers found Willadeane?"

"They have not," he said. "So I'm going to send another officer over to keep an eye on you for the weekend."

"Me?" Meredith asked. "Whatever for?"

"Look," Wally said. "It's Friday, and you and I have spoken more times today than we have in the past two years. Humor me, okay? Another officer should be arriving now. Let him in the back door. He'll do a sweep of the property then hunker down until you're ready to go home. At that point, a surveillance team will take over."

"*Bueno*," Carmen said as she reached down to retrieve the once-full bag of cookies from Meredith's carpet

"And let me repeat, don't eat those cookies. She could have baked anything into them," Wally added. "We will need a forensic analysis. Meredith, make sure you give the officer the cookies and tell him to log them in as evidence."

Carmen threw a cookie back into the crumpled bag and placed it on the table beside the door. "I won't eat them. But someone owes me some cookies when all of this is over."

A half hour later, Meredith's uniformed bodyguard—a fellow who looked like he'd just walked out of a bodybuilding gym—had arrived, the office had been swept, both in terms of looking for Willadeane and also in the literal manner as Meredith used the dust-pan to deposit the last of the cookie crumbs into the evidence bag.

"I'll be out in my car until Detective Parker sends someone to pick up the evidence," the uniformed officer said. "Please don't lock the front door or leave the building until I return. I'll be watching as I do my report."

"I'll make sure she behaves," Carmen said. Her eyes followed the handsome officer as he exited the building.

"Carmen," Julia fussed. "Are you flirting?"

"No way," she said. "He's not my type." She looked over at Meredith. "I prefer the handsome, brainy, history-professor type."

Meredith smiled at the obvious reference to her son Chase, who taught history at Emory University in Atlanta and was more than a little fond of Carmen. "Smart girl," she remarked.

"I'm just wondering what gym he goes to," Carmen said. "I need to start working out, because dieting isn't cutting it."

Julia chuckled. "A half hour ago, you were upset because we took your cookies away from you."

Carmen opened her mouth to offer what Meredith expected would be a sarcastic response. Then she merely shrugged. "I stand by my demand that someone better make good on replacing those cookies. If not you two, then the cops need to take responsibility." She paused. "But I'm totally okay with waiting until after my beach vacation."

Julia turned to go to her office. "Are you really going to the beach?"

"My friend Malia won an all-expenses-paid vacation to Daytona," she said with a grin. "Something to do with selling enough lipstick and eyeliner to get higher in the pyramid than everyone else." Carmen shrugged. "I don't know, exactly, except that I'm her plus-one. She's the friend I've been scouting out a man for. I'm not moving too fast, though. I don't want her to fall in love with the perfect guy and dump me as her plus-one on the trip."

"I do see your dilemma," Meredith said with a poorly disguised grin.

Carmen reached over to take the broom and dustpan from Meredith. "Seriously, though, are you going to be okay alone this weekend, what with Willadeane still on the loose as the suspect in a potential murder attempt? If you need me to, I can come camp out at your place and keep you company."

"Thank you, Carmen," Meredith said, "but I'll be fine. I was supposed to go to a Junior League fundraiser tomorrow, but I'm going to cancel and stay home. If I change my mind, I promise to call you."

"Okay, but remember it's the first Saturday of the month. Harmony and I are going on the Hike for Bikes charity hike unless it's too cold. If it is, then we'll go over to the mall and walk."

As part of a program to mentor girls in at-risk situations through the Boys & Girls Club, Carmen mentored six-year-old Harmony on a regular basis. Her soft heart was just one of the things Meredith and Julia loved about her.

"Mall walking is dangerous," she continued, "what with Cinnabon and the pet store and all, but Harmony's pretty happy either place."

"I won't forget." Meredith paused. "I'm planning for a boring weekend of going over the last of the Worthington files and trying to make some sense of what I've learned the past few days about the case."

"Those DNA tests ought to be back soon, shouldn't they?" Julia asked.

"Monday is what I was told when I called for Meredith this morning," Carmen supplied. "So what's up with Willadeane? She's surely not a killer. She just can't be."

Meredith exchanged a glance with Julia then returned her attention to Carmen. "That's what we're all trying to figure out. Now how about we send you home early? It's five o'clock somewhere, plus it's Friday."

Carmen grinned. "I know you're trying to get rid of me so you and Julia can talk privately, and I'm totally okay with that. I know I'll get the scoop soon enough. Just let me clarify that, like the last time I got to leave early, you're still paying me until five."

"Unless you continue to stand there and procrastinate, yes."

"Message received. *Hasta la vista,* boss ladies. Have a great weekend!"

Chapter Sixteen

A FEW MINUTES LATER THE back door closed and the lock clicked. Finally Meredith and Julia were alone in the office. The silence was deafening.

And absolutely wonderful.

Meredith leaned back in her chair and let out a long breath. Silence fell between them as Julia went out into the hall to pour a cup of coffee for each of them.

She returned and placed a mug in front of Meredith then took a seat across from her. Dappled sunlight stretched across the rug and lit the room in warm light. Beyond the porch, she could see the officer in his squad car.

By degrees, Meredith felt herself relax.

"Meredith! Are you still there?" A man's voice broke the silence.

Meredith yelped and nearly slid off her chair. Julia's hand jerked, sending a wave of coffee to the rug below. She grabbed a handkerchief out of the purse she'd deposited at her side and went down on all fours to handle the damage.

"Wally?" Meredith said, her heart racing. "Why are you still on the phone?"

"Sorry about that." His tone was sheepish as he continued. "I got busy doing paperwork and ignored what was coming out of my phone. Truth be told, I heard it as chatter just like I would the radio when I was a beat cop. If my number wasn't being called, I learned to tune it out."

"Wonderful," Meredith said as she calmed her racing heart.

"Yeah, so I just picked up my phone to make a call and saw I was still on speaker with you. My intention was to apologize and hang up, but I guess I went about it the wrong way."

"You are forgiven," Meredith said. "But you might as well say hello to Julia Foley before you say goodbye."

"Hey, Judge," he called. "Long time no see in court."

"I'm retired now," she said, her head popping up from her work of cleaning coffee off the rug.

"I tried that retirement thing once," he said, his tone jovial. "Hated it. I had to go find something to do. That's how I ended up carrying a badge again."

Julia climbed to her feet, her brown-stained handkerchief in hand. "Sometimes that post-retirement job can be fun." She paused only a moment. "Other times it makes you wonder why you didn't decide to stay home even if the most exciting thing is the day's crossword puzzle."

"Hey," Meredith said to Julia's retreating back. "I like doing crossword puzzles."

"So do I," Wally said.

"Anyway, I know you must be busy with that paperwork, Wally," Meredith said. "Thank you for the quick response. We sure do appreciate you. I imagine we'll be talking again soon. The Savannah PD is the best."

"Glad to help, Meredith."

She hung up and stuck the phone in her purse. By the time Julia came back, Meredith had retrieved her notebook and was ready to debrief her partner on the events of the afternoon—prior to their visit from the police.

"What a day," Julia said. "But I have the distinct feeling I've only heard part of it."

Meredith cast a glance down at her purse to double-check and make sure her phone was not still connected to Wally Parker's line at the police department. She also looked to be sure the ringer was turned on.

"You know the basics. Here's what I didn't tell you on the phone."

After filling her in on the lengthy details of her visit with Sunny, including her allegation that Trey had an early marriage that ended in divorce, Meredith paused. "All she said was, it wasn't her story, and she wasn't at liberty to tell me anything to do with a rose. Evidently, that's Trey's story."

"About Kenneth," Julia said. "I'm trying not to land with Carmen on this one. I just can't imagine Willadeane trying to run him down to increase her share of the inheritance. As a judge I was asked to determine guilt or innocence, and while the impression the defendant gave wasn't always a factor—some are excellent liars—I could generally get to a comfortable verdict after hearing all the testimony and speaking with the person. I've read Willadeane's file, and we've spoken with her at length. I'm reserving judgment until all the facts are in about her car, but I don't think she ran down Kenneth."

"Nor do I," Meredith said. "But when she surprised me in my office with the bag of cookies and Carmen wasn't anywhere around,

I panicked. We don't know her well enough to know what she is capable of, her works of kindness with the elderly aside."

"True," Julia said. "But let's think about this a minute. If Willadeane didn't do it—and I have to admit that her owning a 1971 Eldorado convertible like the one in the police description is far too coincidental—then who did?" She paused. "And yes, I realize this is beyond the scope of our investigation, but I can't help but think about it."

"I've got to defer to Sunny. I think it's possible Kenneth owes someone money." At Julia's doubtful look, Meredith continued. "I know. His parents are loaded. But Sunny was adamant that she raised her children to be independent. She also said Chip offered Kenneth help but he turned it down."

"So that leaves us where?"

"Confused," Meredith said. "It leaves us confused. Or at least me."

"And another visit with Kate won't help?" Julia offered.

"I truly don't know," she said. "They're not on good terms, and not just from what she told us at her office. Sunny basically said the same thing. Kate has the high standard of independence that was drilled into her by her mother, and though Kenneth apparently has his own version of independence, if he won't take Chip's help, it's not sufficient success to meet Kate's expectations. Or that's my guess, at least."

"It's a good guess." Julia paused. "Let's move on to Trey. Have you checked into this elopement?"

"No," Meredith said. "If there were no children, it doesn't matter."

"Agreed," Julia said. "But who's to say there were none? Besides, I am curious."

Meredith shrugged. "I can answer that curiosity with a few clicks of a mouse, Julia." She navigated through the sites until she found what she was looking for. "Okay, here it is. A marriage license for Thomas Daniel Worthington III and Stella Ruth Batson." She shook her head. "You've got to be kidding."

"What?" Julia leaned closer. "Do you know her?"

"Yes, and you do too. Stella Ruth Batson is now Stella Fields. As in Mrs. Anson Fields."

"The congressman?" Julia sat back. "No, really? Stella Fields had a quick elopement with Trey Worthington before she snagged Anson Fields? That's just too much."

"Elopement and divorce," she corrected. "Sunny said Theo Sr. handled it. Marriage license issued in June of 1993 and divorce finalized August 1993."

"Those two had quite a summer vacation," Julia said.

Meredith exhaled a long breath and then pressed PRINT on the page detailing the two events. "I have never been so glad to get my boys past the teen years. They did some outlandish things, but I can't imagine dealing with something as impetuous as an on-the-fly marriage. These two were eighteen years old and had both just graduated high school what appears to be weeks before."

Julia shrugged. "It was an unfortunate choice for both of them, but Stella appears to have done just fine in spite of it. I saw a piece on the *Morning Show* just this morning about the Fieldses' daughter, Rose. Her album just hit number one on the Billboard country music chart."

"Rose," Meredith repeated, eyes wide. "Do you think that's the rose Maggie Lu told us about?"

"It could be," Julia said with glee. "Although I've certainly never heard anything about her being a Worthington. Have you?"

"Never," Meredith said, her mind reeling.

"All right, then. What do you know about Rose Fields?"

"I remember her when she was a deb at the Christmas Cotillion," Meredith said. "Such a pretty girl. I think Chase was smitten with her, but then most of the boys were. He came home from college thinking he'd be the one escorting her to the event. Apparently they'd carried on some kind of flirtation across the miles." She grinned. "However, my son was not the only one who arrived in Savannah that Christmas season thinking to escort Rose Fields to the cotillion. If I remember right, she ended up going with some kid who went on to play quarterback at Alabama. It was quite the scandal, what with her parents being season-ticket-holding Georgia Bulldog fans."

"Oh no, Meredith. That must have been heartbreaking for Chase."

She lifted a shoulder. "A whole group of similarly affected possible escorts for Rose ended up spending the weekend down at the island, fishing and complaining about women. Or so the story was presented to Ron and me by Carter after the fact. He always did love getting his brother in trouble."

"That's what siblings do," Julia said. "So let's tie this in to our heir search. Trey and Stella had a valid marriage from June to August of 1993, correct?"

"That's what the state of Georgia says right here," Meredith said.

"Okay. As long as they didn't have any issue, there is no bearing on our search. Let's confirm when Rose Fields was born, just to make sure there aren't any more surprises down this rabbit trail."

"Oh, speaking of." Meredith cringed as she clicked through to do a search for Rose Fields's birth certificate. "You'll never believe what I said to Sunny. She was going on and on about…" She froze as the document loaded on the screen in front of her. "Julia."

"What?"

"Name: Rose Jane Eliza Fields. Mother's maiden name: Stella Batson. Father: Anson Stephenson Fields III. Date of birth…"

"Meredith, do not leave me hanging," Julia said. "When was she born?"

She met Julia's anxious gaze. "February 12, 1994."

"Oh."

"Yes," Meredith said. "Oh, indeed. Stella married Trey eight months before she gave birth to Rose." She let out a long breath. "But how did she manage to hide this from the prying eyes of the Atlanta social matrons? I don't remember any sort of fuss, but then I was trying to keep up with raising two rambunctious boys, so I didn't pay a lot of attention to that sort of thing back then."

Meredith navigated back to the previous site and did a search for a marriage license between Anson and Stella. "Interesting," she said. "Their marriage license is dated September 1993."

"Meredith," Julia said. "Do we have another possible heir?"

She groaned. "I think we may. I know how you feel about requiring a DNA test, but that's the only way we'll know with any certainty."

"I agree with you, but I'm hesitant to approach Rose about all this. What if she's never been told anything about Trey Worthington and her possible connection to his family? We could be opening up a whole new can of worms unnecessarily if she turns out not to be a blood relation to the Worthingtons. Surely she would have already come forward if she felt she had any claim to the inheritance."

"And yet we have a contract that says we will certify that the heirs we designate are the only heirs to the Worthington trust and that there are no names missing from the list." Meredith sat back. "How do you propose we do that when we now know there's a possibility that Rose Fields is Trey's heir?"

"Since we can't go to Trey, I think we need to go to Rose's mother." Julia paused. "I wonder how Maggie Lu knew."

"There's only one way to find out." Meredith retrieved her phone and dialed Maggie Lu's number.

Maggie Lu picked up on the second ring. After exchanging greetings and explaining that she had Julia on speaker with her, Meredith got to the point of her call.

"I'm sorry to bother you, but Julia and I are sort of in a quandary about something, and I wonder if you have a minute to talk it over with us. It's regarding the Worthington matter."

"Of course," Maggie Lu said. "How can I help?"

"As best we can surmise, Rose Fields was conceived during the time that Stella was married to Trey, but we don't have any confirmation that he's her biological father. If he is, and if he's dead, she's an heir to the Worthington trust."

"I see." There was silence on the other end of the phone. "I wish I had that answer," Maggie Lu said. "I don't."

"Maggie Lu," Julia said. "How did you know about the marriage and Rose's birth? I assume you knew all of that, because you don't sound surprised."

"I told you I had a friend, Effie, who worked for the Worthingtons. After old Mrs. Worthington passed, Tommy Two hired Effie to cook for him. It ended up being a bit more, because the way she told it, she practically raised Trey, what with him loving her cooking. They spent many long hours in her kitchen with her putting plates of food in front of him just to keep him talking. Effie worried about the boy, that she did, but then, as you can see, he gave her good reason to be concerned."

Maggie Lu fell silent again. Then she continued. "By the time Trey went off and married that girl, Effie's daughter had taken her place as the cook while Effie went into retirement. The Worthingtons put her into a pretty little cottage not far from the one on Lombard Street that Ben's family was in for a short time. They owned several houses in that neighborhood and used them to help folks. I know." She chuckled. "They helped others but didn't treat family with as much kindness. I can't explain it, but that's a fact."

"A sad fact," Meredith said. "So Effie continued to feed Trey, I assume."

"She did," Maggie Lu said. "He'd show up with treats for her and whatever set of problems he needed to have worked out. She'd whip up something for him to eat, and they'd go at solving whatever it was he had on his mind."

"And he told her about Rose?"

"No, he told her about Stella, only he didn't admit which girl it was he was thinking of running off with. Said he was taking her out of a situation he didn't think she ought to be in. Never once did he say he wanted to be married to her. Only that he planned to be. Effie was careful in saying that."

"Why did you tell me to ask Sunny about her?" Meredith asked. "How did she know about all of this?"

"Trey's mama was in the middle of battling cancer," Maggie Lu said, "and his daddy was busy trying to keep his head above water while he handled his business and worried about his wife. Sunny, she was an aunt by marriage, but she tried her best to be a sort of mama to him too. I don't blame her for not stopping him. What I do blame her for is helping him keep the secret of that baby after. Trey's daddy should've been told, especially since he helped Trey with the divorce. I promise you, Tommy Two went to his grave not realizing he had a granddaughter, and that's on Trey."

"Okay," Julia said. "I see your point. We found evidence that Stella was married again in September. Do you know anything about that?"

"Not a thing beyond the fact that it happened just like you said," she said. "Though I do find that strange, don't you?"

"A little bit," Meredith agreed. "Seems like 1993 was a year for weddings for her. Normally there aren't two of them within four months, though."

"I wish I could be of more help," Maggie Lu said.

"You've helped plenty," Meredith told her.

"Yes, thank you," Julia added.

After they discussed the baby shower and how Clarissa was progressing in her pregnancy, Julia and Meredith bade Maggie Lu goodbye. Meredith once again tucked the phone into her purse and regarded her partner.

"Wow," she said for lack of a better response. "Now what?"

"Now we speak to Stella," Julia said. "Don't you think? I would rather go to her first than try to explain to Rose the series of events surrounding her conception."

"Especially since we aren't one hundred percent sure what that series of events is," Meredith added. "Only a DNA test can answer that with any certainty."

"Do you think Rose realizes she could be Trey Worthington's daughter?" Julia asked.

"She might," Meredith said. "Or she might not. I think she must not, though, or else she'd be working to claim her share of the inheritance. And I certainly don't want to be the one to tell her, even if she is an adult. Not without giving Stella the opportunity first." Meredith paused to consider their options. "You know, I think I'll go to that fundraiser tomorrow after all."

"Why?" Julia asked, her brow furrowed.

"Because it's being held at Stella's house." Meredith smiled. "Want to be my plus-one?"

"I can't," Julia said. "Beau and I already have weekend plans. But don't forget you've got a plus-one waiting for you in the squad car."

Meredith groaned. "I forgot about him." Then she shrugged. "Oh well. I hope he's got a nice tennis outfit to go along with his uniform. The fundraiser is a tennis tournament out at Stella's place on Moon River."

Chapter Seventeen

STELLA FIELDS SMILED AT MEREDITH over the rim of her iced tea glass as they sat together beneath the broad veranda of her home on a sunny and mild Saturday morning. "If I'd known you were bringing your own tennis pro, Meredith, I would have insisted on having him on my team."

Thus far her police escort—currently undercover in tennis whites and bearing the assumed identity of Larry, an old friend of a friend of Ron's from the force—had won every doubles match in which he'd participated. If fake Larry kept at it, he'd be bringing the Junior League Tennis Championship trophy back to the squad room when this assignment was over.

"He said he loved to play, so I figured he'd enjoy the fundraiser. But I didn't think you played, Stella," Meredith said.

Though she was only in her forties, Stella had that ageless look of preserved plastic that some women liked. It was hard to imagine her doing anything more strenuous than arguing with a caterer over the quality of the imported ingredients in her beef bourguignon.

"I don't," she said with a grin. "I prefer to avoid anything that will cause me to perspire or ruin my makeup—unless I'm paying my trainer to cause it, that is. These thighs don't stay thin by themselves."

Meredith mustered a smile. "No, I suppose not. But I do agree with you. I sweat enough just getting to and from my car most months in this city, so actually taking up an activity that would cause it? I'd have to think long and hard before I'd do that. Of course, gardening my window boxes has the same effect, so who am I to judge?"

"You always have the prettiest window boxes. Who do you use?"

"Myself," Meredith said. "I wasn't kidding when I said that maintaining my flower boxes is my chosen outdoor activity."

Stella's expression went blank as she tucked a strand of hair behind her ear. "I see."

Time to move the conversation along. "Stella, I was wondering if we could speak in private."

"This is private," she said. "What's up? Do you finally have a suggestion for next year's social committee chair? I'm at my wit's end trying to decide. There just isn't a wide enough group of candidates to choose from."

Meredith paused to glance around. The majority of the guests, numbering at least three dozen, were seated or standing around the tennis court watching Larry and whoever had lucked out into being his partner this time around, but a few were speaking in clusters near the water or wandering too close for comfort.

"Inside, maybe?"

"Oh." She gave Meredith a knowing look. "You don't want anyone to know who you're endorsing. I understand."

"It's true what I have to say isn't something I want overheard," Meredith managed, skirting Stella's assumption.

Stella waved at a uniformed waiter, and he hurried to her side. "Circulate more, please. This food won't keep well in the freezer, and that's exactly what Mr. Fields will want to do with it if it's not all eaten." She looked over at Meredith and shrugged. "He loves leftovers. It's a quirk of his. I can't explain it."

Her hostess returned her attention to the waiter. "I'll just be a minute. I've got to take a quick meeting with Mrs. Bellefontaine. Has my daughter arrived?"

"About ten minutes ago," he told her.

"Wonderful." She rose and nodded to Meredith. "Come with me, and we'll chat. Then, if Rose isn't being too much of a hermit, I'll introduce you."

Meredith followed Stella into a waterfront home that was the exact opposite of the one Sunny owned. Rather than an interior of creamy whites, this home was done in a riot of colors.

Stella stepped onto leopard-print carpet that marched down a hallway hung with modern art that looked like a toddler had been playing with finger paints. "We can use Anson's study," she said. "He's conveniently in Atlanta this weekend. Something to do with a budget meeting. If you ask me, it's because he knew the event would be mostly women and he didn't want to make polite conversation. Plus, he's a terrible tennis player, but don't tell him I told you that."

"Your secret is safe with me."

They stepped into a room that looked as if it belonged in an English country manor. Every surface was covered in some sort of dark fabric, from the green silk on the walls and windows to the dark blue fabric dotted with gold fleur-de-lis on the wing chairs. A print of a fox hunt was hung over a fireplace mantel made of carved ebony, and a half-dozen heads of exotic animals were hung on the opposite wall.

"Wow," Meredith said.

"I know." Stella sashayed over to the massive carved rosewood desk and plopped down in the creaky leather chair, twirling a bleach-blond strand of hair around her finger and affecting a pout that Meredith was sure she used often. "Anson is impossible. He told me I could decorate the house however I wanted, but his study was off limits."

"It does look like you used a different designer in here," Meredith managed.

"His *mother* is responsible for this horror. I try not to imagine what this room would look like with the walls painted a bright color and some nice art hung everywhere. Maybe a hanging plexiglass chair. I love those."

Meredith also tried not to imagine it as she took a seat on the chair across from Stella. "If you don't mind, I'd rather just get right to business."

"Sure," Stella said with a shrug. "Who's the candidate you're recommending?"

"Actually, I'm not recommending a candidate. I need to talk to you about Rose." Before Stella could comment, Meredith continued. "Specifically in regard to Trey Worthington."

Her eyes widened. Then abruptly narrowed.

"There's nothing to discuss."

"But there is," Meredith protested gently. "Magnolia Investigations has been charged with doing our due diligence in regard to verifying all legal claimants to the Worthington inheritance, and we're hoping to get a DNA sample from Rose. But before we approach her, I wanted to speak with you first. You see, we cannot, in good conscience, ignore the fact that your daughter might be—"

"Enough, Meredith," Stella said. "As I said, there is nothing to be discussed. It has been handled."

"I fail to see how you can say that," Meredith said, her patience growing thin. "There's a real possibility we'll be missing an heir if we return our report without—"

Stella stood and laid her palms on Anson's desk. "Okay, I get it. You have your job to do. Well, Meredith, I have mine. And I have handled it."

"How?" Meredith demanded as she rose to face her.

"You'll have your DNA sample results on Monday," she said. "You can talk to Theo about the details. If you must know, he has already handled everything."

"So you told Rose about Trey?"

"No. I'll cross that bridge if I have to."

"If we find proof that Trey is dead and Rose is next in line for the inheritance, you'll have to," Meredith warned. "But I need to know more about how this DNA test was conducted."

"If you must know, I sent Rose to Theo last week to have him look over some estate planning documents he'd drafted. She's young, but she needs to think about these things. We all do." Stella shrugged. "I had prearranged it all with Theo. A bottle of water that his intern took away before Rose could take it with her did the trick. I know the results of this kind of a DNA sample may not stand up in court, if it ever comes to that, but under the circumstances, it seemed like the least intrusive way to get this handled. We'll take any other steps that are necessary when we get to that point."

"Okay, then I guess I'll wait to hear the results on Monday." Meredith paused. "You don't have to answer this, but I'm curious, so I'll ask. Why did you get married twice in 1993?"

"One for love and the other because I thought I had to. I'll leave it to you to figure out which was which. Now let's go see if your friend Larry is going to take home the trophy. They ought to be playing the finals by now."

Later, after "Friend of a Friend Larry" had made a moving speech about how much winning the annual Junior League tennis trophy would be changing his life—and Meredith assumed he intentionally left out any hint that his fellow officers likely would be chiding him for weeks over the "rough duty" he'd undertaken over the weekend—he drove Meredith home.

They had just arrived there when the officer's phone rang. After a moment of conversation, he hung up. "They got her, Mrs. Bellefontaine. The Worthington lady is in custody, so I guess this is goodbye."

Meredith smiled, though her feelings about jailing Willadeane Worthington were ambivalent at best. "Thank you for letting me know. And congratulations on your trophy."

He grinned. "Anytime you need a bodyguard, I'm your guy."

"I'll keep that in mind."

Meredith watched him drive away and then went inside, relief flooding her. The rest of the weekend—what was left of it—would at least be spent in solitude, now that her shadow had taken his trophy and gone.

She dropped her purse and keys on the table by the door and then kicked off her shoes. Her cat, GK, wandered halfway down the stairs to give her a look that told her exactly how her entrance had ruined his nap.

"Sorry about that, pal. Some of us have to work for a living," she said as she padded toward the kitchen.

Flicking on the switch for the overhead lights, Meredith stopped short. In the middle of the island was a plain white envelope with her first name printed on it in crude block letters.

It hadn't been there when she left.

This wasn't Chase's handwriting or Carter's, nor did his wife, Sherri Lynn, write it. Meredith would have recognized the way they formed their letters, and any of them would have referred to her as Mom not Meredith.

The string of vowels and consonants weren't childlike—and it spelled her given name, which was not what her grandchildren called her. Thus it wasn't likely that her grandchildren, Kaden and Kinsley, were responsible.

Plus, if any of them were intent on paying a visit, wouldn't they have called first?

The implication struck her, and Meredith's heart lurched. She patted her pocket and realized her phone was in her purse. Retracing her steps, her eyes searching for any sign of an intruder, she went back to the door, slipped into her shoes, and retrieved her purse, keys, and phone.

After hurrying outside, she locked the door and walked out to the street. With trembling hands, she hit REDIAL on Wally Parker's phone number.

He answered on the second ring. "I'm sorry to call you on a Saturday, Wally, but I think I've had an intruder." She told him what she'd found.

"Where are you now? If you're in the house, get out."

"I'm not," she said. "I'm standing out here in front of the house. I locked it back up and walked out as soon as I realized what I was looking at. And before you ask, I didn't touch the envelope. For that matter, all I touched was the doorknob on the front door—both sides—and the light switch in the kitchen."

"Okay, stay put. You know the drill."

"I do," she said. "And I will."

Her next call was to Julia. "So, interesting day I'm having." As soon as the words were out, she recalled that her partner had weekend plans with her husband. "But I'll tell you all about it on Monday. I know you're with Beau, but I wanted to let you know that Stella beat us to it and arranged a DNA test for Rose. The results will be ready on Monday."

"I'm sure that's an interesting story. I wonder who tipped her off."

"My guess is all the news coverage of the Worthington trust finally being distributed caused her to react. It's no secret that we're investigating."

"We've been mentioned in a couple of reports, so I guess that makes sense."

"One other update. Willadeane has been apprehended."

"That makes me sad, Meredith." Julia paused. "And relieved all at the same time."

"I know. Me too." Meredith glanced up to see two Savannah police cruisers barreling around the corner, lights flashing and sirens blaring. "I'm giving you back to Beau now. Enjoy your weekend. I'll talk to you on Monday, okay? Bye!"

Chapter Eighteen

"MEREDITH BELLEFONTAINE! WHEN DID YOU plan to tell me that when you called on Saturday the sirens I heard in the background were heading to your house?"

The question, spoken in Julia's voice, echoed down the corridor of the building. A moment later, she appeared in the doorway to Meredith's office and leaned against the doorframe, arms folded.

"I'm sorry," Meredith said. "But there was no reason to interrupt a perfectly nice weekend with your husband to tell you that some creep left an envelope in my kitchen."

"Any idea who?"

"None," she said. "There was no sign of forced entry. I had the alarm system checked and the locks changed before I went to bed Saturday night."

Julia gave her a horrified look. "You slept there alone?"

"Wally insisted on having an officer outside, but yes, I was alone inside. And before you ask, no, I did not tell Quin any of this. We're friends, and I think there's something there between us, but I'm not ready to put him in the position of taking care of me. And I haven't told the boys. They'd be beside themselves and likely drive me crazier than I already feel." She paused. "Am I making any sense?"

"Plenty." Julia glanced over her shoulder. "Where's Carmen?"

"She went down to Theo's office to check on the DNA results from the heirs. I told her to hang around and wait if they thought the results would be coming soon." She sat back in her chair. "The good news is I finished the last of the boxes from Theo. I can say with absolute certainty that there are no new heirs among those who contacted the law firm. Not a one of them panned out as being remotely related."

"That's a relief." Julia reached into her pocket and retrieved her phone. "I'll text Carmen and ask her to have someone come pick up the boxes." She typed out a message, pressed SEND, and then looked back up at Meredith. "Have you heard anything about Willadeane? Other than that she was picked up on Saturday?"

"Nothing."

"Truly, Meredith. Do you think she would do what she's accused of?"

Meredith let out a long breath. "I don't know. I'll trust whatever the police decide. Money is a strong motivator."

Julia nodded. "I just realized that you never said what was in the envelope."

"Oh, that." Meredith forced herself to speak calmly. "It said 'I want my money.'"

"Lovely. And I suppose there was no signature." Julia's phone dinged, and she jumped.

"None," Meredith said. "Wally is hoping to find prints, but I figure he would have called by now if he had."

Julia looked up from her phone. "It's Carmen. She said the intern is on his way back from the lab. Apparently these sorts of things are done by hand and not mailed. So she's waiting around until he returns. Should be soon."

Meredith sat very still, her thoughts racing. Kenneth was missing. Willadeane was likely still in police custody until they could determine whether or not it was her car involved in the hit-and-run. And someone wanted in on the Worthington trust enough to try and intimidate her by breaking into her home and leaving a message.

The only heirs left untouched by all of this mess were Trey—if he was, in fact, alive—and Kate. It was likely that Meredith could rule out Kate based on how little interest the Worthington twin had shown in receiving funds from the trust.

Considering that, according to the *Savannah Morning News*, Kate's husband had just inked a lucrative deal to do commentary for the NFL and she was likely well paid in her on-air position at WSVG, it was unlikely she would be willing to intimidate or commit attempted murder to increase her portion.

That left Trey. Who might be dead. Or might be alive and incognito. What better place to hide than right in plain sight?

But not in his hometown. That would be ridiculous.

And what if his cousin Kate was intentionally trying to put them off the scent? What if she was fully aware of the substantial amount of the inheritance—the media was certainly speculating and the numbers weren't that far off—and she wanted it badly enough to do something like this to get it?

"Meredith?"

She shook off her rambling thoughts. "Sorry, I was trying to put the pieces of this puzzle together. I'm not sure it can be done."

"Carmen just texted me. She's on her way with the results." Julia paused. "You were saying you're trying to put the pieces together."

Meredith exhaled slowly. "I was trying to look at the possible heirs and figure out which of them was capable of killing to get a higher share, but I can make a case for all of them." She paused. "And I can think of a good reason for each of them as to why it couldn't possibly be them. See, it's impossible."

"Well," Julia said slowly, "the good news is that we don't have to solve the question of who committed the hit-and-run crime against Kenneth, and we don't have to identify the person or persons who broke into your home and left that envelope. Those crimes are the responsibility of the Savannah PD."

"True."

"So we've investigated and we've now put our faith in science. Let's see what science tells us, shall we?" She paused. "And in the meantime, I'm going to make another call to see if I can't expedite our investigation into the whereabouts of Trey Worthington."

"Or whether he's alive," Meredith added.

"Right. Well, I'm going to stick with whereabouts until proven otherwise."

Her footsteps faded down the hall. Meredith sat back and watched the swing swaying in the breeze on the porch outside her window. It was another lovely day, and that swing seemed to call to her.

"Why not?" she muttered. "I can't concentrate on anything until Carmen gets back with the results."

She tucked her phone into her pocket and called to Julia. "I'll be out on the swing if you need me."

Meredith closed the door behind her and settled into her favorite spot. From here she could see up and down Whitaker Street. She also had a nice view of Forsyth Park beyond the small hedge and the rows of azaleas. The officer assigned to watch her after the envelope incident rolled his window down when he noticed her.

"Everything all right, ma'am?" the young man asked.

"Just enjoying the weather," she told him with a wave of her hand. "I'm fine."

Her phone buzzed, and she pulled it from her pocket. The message was from Wally: WILLADEANE WORTHINGTON RELEASED FROM CUSTODY. MY GUT SAYS YOU'RE SAFE AND SHE'S INNOCENT BUT WILL ALERT THE OFFICER OF THE SITUATION.

Meredith paused only a moment and then responded: I DON'T THINK SHE DID THIS.

He responded immediately: NEITHER DO I.

A few minutes later, Julia opened the door. "Carmen's back. The results are on my desk." She paused. "And no, I didn't look at them yet."

Meredith stood and followed Julia back inside. The envelope from Theo's firm sat on the desk between them as Meredith settled into a chair across from Julia.

"Go ahead," Meredith said. "Open it and read the results."

Julia reached for the envelope just as her phone rang. "It's the man I've been trying to talk to about Trey."

"Then you better answer it," Meredith said. "The results will wait a few more minutes."

Julia answered and pressed SPEAKER mode. "Thank you for calling me back," she said. "I appreciate that you're in a difficult spot, but so are we."

"I get it," a woman said, her voice distinctly Southern. "You're a judge, so you know how this works. Disappearing into WITSEC means you no longer exist. That's just how it is."

"And just so I'm clear, once someone disappears into WITSEC, that decision can be reversed, right?"

"By the government, no."

"So there's no way out?" Julia asked.

"Just one," the woman said. "There is no obligation to stay in WITSEC. The person who elected to go into protection can use the default clause and leave it at any time."

Julia exchanged glances with Meredith. "So if a situation changed, say a family member died or there was a large inheritance out there for him, then that person could leave WITSEC and resume his old life."

"That is never a good idea. Remember, these people have very good reasons to disappear."

"I understand that," she said, "but don't you think Trey would want to make that choice?"

Silence fell between them.

Finally the woman spoke. "I cannot confirm or deny whether Mr. Worthington is in a position to make this decision."

"So you're saying he's alive?"

"That isn't what I'm saying at all."

"Can someone in WITSEC have a visitor from their previous life?"

"I've never heard of anything like that happening," the woman said. "And it's possible that would invoke the default clause."

Julia sighed. "Okay, I know I'm putting you on the spot, and I apologize. I would like to just try one more thing. You don't have to confirm or deny anything, but I would like to get word to Trey that Meredith Bellefontaine and I would like to meet with him on his terms at his choice of time and location."

"Should this be possible, what reason will he be given for this meeting?"

Julia reached for the envelope, tore it open, and then looked down at the page she pulled out. "Tell him it may concern the possibility of a biological daughter." She paused. "And if he is alive and he tells you he doesn't have one, DNA says otherwise. She was born in 1994."

"I can't promise anything," the woman said. "And if you do hear from anyone, it won't be me."

Julia dropped the paper on her desk. So Rose was genetically a Worthington. But what about Willadeane? With Julia still on the phone, Meredith couldn't bring herself to look.

"I understand. And thank you," Julia said.

The line clicked as the call ended. Julia looked over at Meredith.

"I'm sorry for opening the envelope the way I did, Meredith. I felt like we were losing any option to get him to respond if he's alive. Learning you have a daughter could be a pretty powerful motive."

Meredith nodded. "No, you did the right thing. Obviously, Trey walked away from a lot of money even before the Worthington trust came into question. He's Tommy Two's only heir. He needed a different motivation to let us talk to him, if he is, in fact, alive."

Julia's gaze fell to the paper and then returned to meet Meredith's gaze. "Did you look at the results yet?"

Meredith shook her head.

"You better brace yourself."

"Why?" Meredith picked up the paper. "Other than the surprise that Rose might be an heir, that is."

Julia's expression was grave. "Just look."

Meredith read the results. Then read them again.

Slowly her attention went from the page to Julia.

"Well," she said, "Kenneth and Kate are confirmed. And Rose. Oh Julia, is there any way that last one could be wrong?"

She stared at the final result. Willadeane Worthington had failed to prove her claim, regardless of what was reported in the first set of results she had provided. She was not a biological member of the Worthington family.

She was not Simon's heir.

Julia's phone rang again. She snatched it up while Meredith continued to gape at the results.

"On our way." She ended the call and clutched the phone in her hand. "Grab your purse."

"Why, where are we going?"

Julia grinned. "Jekyll Island. And that's all I'm telling you until we get in the car."

✎ Chapter Nineteen ✎

MEREDITH STEPPED OUT OF JULIA'S car and glanced around. Davis Charters was located in what was pretty much a reclaimed FEMA trailer perched in a parking lot that edged the water. Beyond the lot was a fishing boat tied to a dock that had seen its better days and, on the other side of the channel, Jekyll Island.

Julia knocked on the door of the trailer then turned around to give Meredith a frustrated look as she held up a small slip of paper. "The sign says the owner has gone fishing."

"It is a fishing charter, Julia," she said. "I see a boat. Maybe he's back and hasn't pulled down the sign yet."

"After you," Julia said as she followed Meredith toward the dock.

"Careful," Meredith told her once they reached the ancient bleached wood structure. "There are loose boards and nails sticking out."

"That's on purpose," a masculine voice called. "Come aboard if you can get to me. I'm working on the engine."

Meredith glanced back at Julia and shook her head. Surely this wasn't Trey Worthington. Not the Trey Worthington who made—and apparently lost—a fortune in shady dealings up north.

The fishing boat—a decent-sized vessel with two decks, fishing chairs in back, and the odd name of *Gotcha*—was bobbing and tugging against the rope. Meredith managed to gain solid footing and step down onto the deck. Julia followed, looking less sure of this adventure than she had back in Savannah.

"Where are you?" Meredith called into the darkness that was the interior of the vessel.

"Hold on," the man said. "I'll come up to you."

"Okay," Julia said. "We'll just wait out here." She leaned over to Meredith. "I'm not going down there," she whispered.

Meredith clutched her purse, her licensed weapon at the ready should this turn out to be some kind of trap. Until she stepped onto the boat, she hadn't considered that this whole thing could be a setup.

That the Mob might be behind the demand for money.

And they had someone make the call.

And followed them.

She looked back toward the parking lot. Not a car in sight.

No, they knew where she and Julia were going, so they wouldn't have had to follow. Instead they'd be waiting. Maybe inside that building.

Or down in the hold of this fishing boat.

Her heart galloped. Not a good thing for a woman with previous heart scares. Time to flee.

"Let's go," she hissed at Julia, clutching her arm. "I've got a bad—"

"Hello, Mrs. Bellefontaine, Judge Foley."

Meredith turned around to see a man in a faded Hawaiian shirt, khaki shorts, and a yellow baseball cap emblazoned with a logo for Davis Charters. Bare feet and a tan completed the image.

Indeed, the man standing in the doorway wiping his hands on a mechanic's cloth bore very little resemblance to the New York financier that Tommy Two's son had been. And yet it was him, Thomas Daniel Worthington III.

It was Trey.

He remained in the doorway, hidden from anyone who might be watching from the road, the parking lot, or even the beach behind Meredith. The only way to see the captain of the *Gotcha* was to stand right in front of him.

Which she was doing.

"Trey," Meredith said on a long breath. "You're alive."

He finished wiping his hands and tossed the dirty rag behind him with no notice of where it landed. "No, ma'am," he said. "He's not." Then he paused only for a second before thrusting out his clean hand. "Alan Davis," he told her. "And I'm sorry to hear of your loss."

"Our loss?" Julia shook her head. "I don't understand."

"This man Trey Worthington. He's dead. I'm sorry about that." His expression appeared to beg them to understand though his eyes looked as though he realized they would not. Not yet. "However," he continued, "I understand I look a little bit like him."

Understanding dawned. Even here, now, with no one around, Trey could not relax his guard.

"You do, Mr. Davis. The resemblance is uncanny."

He grinned. "Well, it is now. But I've got this deviated septum that'll get operated on in a few weeks. It's pretty much a nose job, but my doctor says there might be a tweak or two elsewhere."

"Yes," Julia told him. "You'll breathe much better once it's done."

"I will," he told her. "So I believe you had something to show me."

Meredith retrieved the test results from her purse and held it where he could see it. Trey leaned forward to read the results, his gaze lingering there.

Then he looked up, his eyes narrowed. "Your test is wrong."

"I don't think you understand," Julia told him. "If Trey Worthington is, in fact, deceased, his daughter Rose Fields will inherit his portion of Wilhelmina Worthington's trust."

"Oh, I understand all that just fine." He glanced around and then returned his attention to them. "Hold on tight. We're going for a ride."

"Wait a minute," Meredith said. "Why would we do that?"

He leaned in close. "Because nobody can listen in when you're out there."

A half hour later, Trey shut off the engines and anchored the boat. Then he joined them on the deck. "Okay, I'm going to make this quick. But first I need to know if Stella could have done this."

"Done what?" Julia asked.

"Been responsible for those test results," he said.

Meredith thought back to Stella's description of how the DNA sample was acquired. "Possibly," she said. "Although it would be a stretch to say for sure. The sample was acquired from Rose in a law office."

Not exactly aboveboard if Rose was only there to look at estate-planning documents and wasn't aware of providing a sample. She stifled a groan. This would all be an eventuality best investigated on dry land back in Savannah. There was no need to discuss it now.

Trey seemed to accept that answer.

"Okay, so here's the deal," he said. "Yes, I was briefly married to Stella. We were stupid. I thought I was being noble. White knight charging in to save the day and all that. Trouble was, I'd only been married to Stella for a week when she informed me she no longer needed saving."

"What do you mean by saving?" Julia asked.

"When Stella came to me right after graduation and told me she thought she was pregnant, I was pretty surprised. I mean, she hadn't dated anyone regularly that I knew of, and she and I were good friends. If she had a boyfriend, I figured I would know it."

Meredith watched a pair of gulls sweep into the water and then come up again, their bills empty. "Did you ask whose it was, Trey?"

"That was the first thing I asked. She told me it didn't matter, because he refused to take responsibility. As I recall she put on a pretty good show that night. Lots of tears and repeating how her parents would kill her once they found out she was pregnant and unmarried. Stuff like that. I figured what the heck. I can help with that. So I did."

"So, you two secretly fixed the part about her being unmarried," Julia offered.

"Yeah." He grinned, and his teeth gleamed white against his tanned face. "For a short time there, I was Stella's hero. She kept telling me the time wasn't right to tell her parents yet. That we'd tell our folks together soon."

"Did that ever happen?" Julia asked.

"No," he said. "I got so frustrated that I resorted to talking to Sunny about it. I'm guessing she's got something to do with you two finding it all out."

"We can't say," Meredith told him. "How did the divorce come to be?"

"Like I said, our marriage pretty much ended within weeks of when it began. She told me we needed to talk. Never tell a guy that. It terrifies him," he said with a chuckle. "But in this case, it was the release I didn't know I needed. She told me the marriage was over, and we needed a divorce because her baby's father had proposed and she was going to marry him instead."

"Anson Fields," Julia supplied, and he nodded.

"I took care of the divorce. Theo Sr. had been the family lawyer since Granny was in charge, so I went down to his office and took him into my confidence. I was over eighteen—just barely—so he had to keep our meeting secret from my family. He did all the paperwork. I took it to Stella to sign and that was that. I went off to college and then heard through the grapevine that she'd married Fields a week after the divorce was finalized."

"About that," Meredith said. "I don't remember hearing much fuss about it when Stella married Anson. Do you have any idea why?"

"Of course I do. For all her ditzy blond routine, Stella is a sharp businesswoman. She cut a deal with her folks. She wouldn't shame them by telling everyone she was unmarried and pregnant if they made a way for her to marry Anson Fields. With his father's stature in the community and the fact that Stella's folks were professional social climbers, the deal was struck, and everyone got what they wanted."

"Except you?" Julia asked.

"Oh no," Trey told her. "I didn't know it at the time, but I got exactly what I needed. Our cook, Effie, was a second mother to me.

Truth be told, she was more of a mother once my mom got cancer. She told me to shake the dust off and move on, just like they did in the Bible. 'Don't stay where you don't belong,' she would tell me." He looked away. "I wish I'd taken her advice more often."

Silence fell between them, punctuated only by the shrill cry of the gulls and the lap of the waves against the boat's hull. Finally Trey shrugged. "I guess we ought to get back. I promised my handler I wouldn't take more than an hour with you. Apparently it's pretty irregular to get to visit with someone from your old life. But since Judge Foley technically isn't from that life and she's a judge…" He paused. "Well, anyway, I appreciate that you could come on short notice."

"And we appreciate that you were willing to risk speaking to us," Julia said.

"There is one more thing that we need to talk about before we go back in," Meredith said. "The question of whether you're an heir. It's a problem."

"No," he said easily. "It isn't a problem at all. Trey Worthington is dead. Pass my share on to family, but please promise me you'll have that test repeated. And that this time you'll be in the room when it happens so Stella can't manipulate the results."

Meredith gave his request a moment's consideration. "I can do that," she said, "though I have to tell you that Rose doesn't know any of this. She isn't even aware that she was given a test the first time. Her DNA was taken without her knowledge."

"We found this out after the fact," Julia added.

"Again, that has the mark of Stella all over it." He paused. "If the results come out the same, then give it all to Rose. But they won't. I'm certain of it."

"Why?" Julia asked.

"Because we were just friends, nothing more." He paused for emphasis. "That never changed. Nothing ever happened. I absolutely cannot be Rose's father."

Meredith nodded. "I believe you're sincere, Trey. So that begs the question of who would inherit if you aren't alive to be the heir and Rose isn't related biologically. Did you write a will?"

"I did not," he said. "And that is a regret Alan Davis will carry the rest of his life. If it were up to me, I wouldn't want Sunny's kids to have it." He paused. "I'd rather not say why."

"You're not required to say why," Meredith responded.

"Who's that other lady?" he asked. "The one who has Granny's name. I don't know her."

"She's one of the people who claimed a relationship but ultimately wasn't related," Julia said.

"Yeah, I saw that. But you believed her to the point of testing her. Did you do that with anyone else?"

Meredith shook her head.

"Well, too bad she didn't test positive. I'd rather give the money to a stranger than family." Trey shrugged. "That sounds harsh, but I'm a prime example of what too much money can do to an otherwise perfectly normal person. Look what I did just to build up my bank account. I had seven figures in the bank and still partnered with the Mob to get richer."

"Probably not the best idea you've had," Meredith said.

Trey shook his head. "That was dumber than marrying Stella. I couldn't even claim honor or good intentions on that one."

"You've learned a hard lesson," Meredith said.

"Yes, ma'am, and I've been given another chance. I would like to think all those prayers sweet Effie prayed over me got me that do-over." He paused. "I don't want Trey's money or his life. I like being Alan Davis. Look around. He's got a much better view out his office window."

"You've got a point." Meredith paused. "One more thing, Trey. Julia will know more about this than me, but somehow we're going to have to have you declared dead. Or presumed dead. Or something like that." She looked over to Julia for help.

"There is a way to have a presumption of death action filed, but I'll have to look into that," Julia said. "Either way, if you have no children or spouse or legal heirs, then it's a fairly seamless process."

"I have none of those," he said. "And you can take that to the bank."

With that statement, Trey turned and walked back toward the interior of the boat. "Hang on," he called. "It's time to head back in."

The fishing vessel cut through the waves like a speedboat as they went back in toward shore, easily besting the time it took to go out. It was as if Trey Worthington had said his piece and was ready to be done with not only the conversation but the reminder of his previous life.

Once the boat was tied at the dock, Trey paused only a moment. "I'm going back to working on that engine," he said. "I didn't like the knocking I heard when we were coming back in."

"All right," Meredith said. "We'll see ourselves off. Thank you for talking to us."

"Thank you for pushing me to talk to you," he countered.

"The credit for that goes to Julia," Meredith said.

"Just one more thing before you go," Trey said. "I guess if Kate and Kenneth inherit my money, that's fine. We're years apart in age, but I like my cousins well enough. Or I did when we were younger, anyway. But there's something I want you to do before you sort everything out and write those checks."

"What's that?" Julia asked.

He leaned in. "Take a closer look at what Sunny was up to in 1988."

"Planning a wedding, I would think," Meredith told him. "That's how it's normally done, since she got married in 1989."

Trey lifted one brow. "You've been looking into our family for a while. Since when do we do anything the normal way?"

Meredith shook her head. "What are you saying?"

"You'll see." He chuckled. "Theo Sr. fixed that too."

"Fixed what?"

"Nope," he said. "My days as a snitch are over. Trey might have told you everything, but Alan Davis just sort of guides you in the right direction then lets you fish out the answer for yourself." He paused, the beginnings of a smile rising. "Pardon the pun. But when you talk to Sunny about it—and I guarantee you will—be sure to let her know that I have one word for her."

"What's that?"

He lifted a brow. "Gotcha."

Meredith thought about that statement all the way back to the car. As Julia was pulling out, she glanced over to find Trey watching them from the bridge of the *Gotcha*.

She waved, but he didn't respond. Rather, he disappeared from sight, and with him, so did Trey Worthington.

Chapter Twenty

THE NEXT DAY MEREDITH GLANCED around the elegantly appointed conference room of Lucas, Wilson, Kyler & Strong, and sighed. "This office is much fancier than ours."

"It ought to be," Julia said as she shifted positions in the expensive Louis XIV side chair where she'd been told to sit.

Sixteen ornately carved monsters marched around the edge of a highly polished oval table, each figure a study in elegance and torture at the same time. Two silver tea sets divided the middle of the table with a spray of flowers that reached halfway to the coffered mahogany ceiling centered between them.

Real flowers, Meredith noted without the least bit of surprise.

Between the art and the crystal and the silver, just the contents of this room were probably worth more than a year's salary of any of the young lawyers who'd passed them on their way up the grand staircase.

"It's the house that Wilhelmina Worthington built," Meredith added. "And before that, it was her daddy's bank, the Styles Bank and Trust. Nothing but the best for that family and their employees."

The same intern who had introduced himself as Ryan Cole on their way up the staircase returned to the room. Behind him was what could best be described as a waiter carrying a tray of bottled water.

Flashes of the deception allegedly practiced on Rose Fields and actually used with the bottle left in her car by Skate Worthington rose in Meredith's mind. "No, thank you," she said when one was offered to her.

"I have a question," Julia asked the intern. "Bottled water seems a little, well, less formal than this place deserves. I expected I would be offered a pitcher and a glass."

He frowned. "I'm new. Maybe we've got that in the kitchen."

She shook her head. "Never mind."

"I'm fine too," Meredith said.

"All right," Ryan said. "Mr. Lucas will be right with you."

Once the doors closed again, Meredith's eyes narrowed. "Bottles of water on a tray? I'm thinking that intern doesn't have a clue."

Julia giggled. "Careful, Meredith, your society roots are showing."

She laughed. "Okay, but I'm also an investigator, and I notice things. I guarantee if this firm is working this hard to look prosperous, the partners would have a conniption if they knew a client was being offered plastic on a tray."

The door opened, and Theo stepped inside. He had shaved his beard.

"Well now," Meredith said. "You look nice. Six months ahead of schedule, but nice."

Theo grinned and stroked his chin as he seated himself at the head of the table near them. "I've always been a little bit of a rebel. Some of my colleagues are participating in no-shave November. I decided I'd do the opposite."

"It does look very nice," Julia agreed.

"Well, thank you both, ladies. I see here by the meeting notes Ruth prepared for me that you have some questions about the DNA results." He looked up. "Are you disputing them?"

"Not completely," Julia said. "Rather, we are asking for another round of testing to support them."

"You have more possibles?"

"Fewer, we think," Julia said. "But first we want to arrange a more controlled environment in which to conduct the tests. We're not fully comfortable with the four sets of results we received yesterday."

Theo folded his hands in front of him, his brow furrowed. "In what way?"

"In a way that requires us to request new tests," Meredith offered. "If we are to do our due diligence, a repeat is essential. Do you need the details?"

He thought a moment and then said, "All right. I hired you to give me an answer, and I'm not willing to have that answer called into question down the road by a judge because I skimped on a repeat of a test. No, I do not need the details. How do you propose we do this?"

"Call a meeting of each of the prospective heirs. Tell them whatever you want," Julia said. "I would suggest something along the lines of letting them know they are possible heirs and, as such, need to meet with you immediately to discuss the next step."

"Yes, all right."

"Have them all come at the same time," Meredith suggested. "Today, if you can arrange it, or tomorrow."

"That's asking a lot," Trey said.

"You're offering a percentage of a $100 million trust," Julia said. "So they'll be getting a lot."

Theo reached under the desk to press a buzzer. A moment later, Ryan returned along with an older woman.

"Have you ladies met Ruth Felder? She's one of my assistants. And this is one of our new interns, Ryan Cole. I believe you've met."

Dressed very much like Queen Elizabeth, minus the hat and crown jewels, Ruth glanced over at them as if she was surveying her kingdom. Her deep blue eyes matched the color of her tailored dress and were highlighted by a sapphire pin on her lapel in the shape of the letter R.

After greetings were exchanged, Theo continued. "Ruth, please do your magic and get the four heirs who are listed on the Worthington family DNA tests into the office no later than close of business tomorrow. There's a bonus in it for you if they come today. The catch is they have to come at the same time, so be sure all four conference rooms are available."

"Is that all, sir?" she asked in a British accent that sounded straight out of Buckingham Palace.

"I think so," he said. "Thank you."

Ruth turned to go.

"Excuse me, Ms. Felder," Meredith said.

"Yes?"

"Unless things have changed, it's possible that Kenneth Worthington may still be missing. Since his sister is authenticated as his twin, I believe Julia and I would be willing to allow whatever test result Kate gets to apply to both of them."

"Yes," Julia said. "That makes sense."

"And one more thing. Rose Fields was duped into unknowingly taking a DNA test here in your office." Meredith looked over at Theo. "We understand you had something to do with that?"

His expression remained stoic and unreadable. "Where did you hear that?"

"Her mother," Meredith said. "So when Ruth makes the appointment, I propose she schedule it with Stella. Let Mom be the one to tell Rose about her possible inheritance and the situation surrounding it."

"That situation being what?" Theo asked.

"I'd rather not say at this point," Meredith told him. "It would only be conjecture. But suffice to say we have reason to include her."

He nodded. "And I trust it is a good reason, though I wondered where her name came in to play in this situation. Anson Fields has been a client for years, and I'm not aware of any direct link between his family and the Worthingtons."

"Another reason for a controlled environment for the test," Julia said. "And for her mother to handle the reason for the meeting."

"Let me talk to Stella," Theo said. "You give me the day and time that the others are coming in, and I will see that she's here with Rose."

"So let me get this straight," Ruth said, the royal gaze falling back on Theo. "I call the Worthington twins but Kate first, and maybe Kenneth can't be here, but that's okay." At Meredith and Julia's nods, she continued. "Then I reach out to Willadeane Worthington and get her here, all whilst arranging for DNA tests times four."

"Yes," Theo said. "With expedited results. Whatever it costs."

"Of course," she said as if Theo had just asked her to slap at an errant housefly rather than to arrange what clearly sounded like the impossible—and on short notice. "And you will settle the details for Stella and Rose Fields to attend, Mr. Lucas?"

"Yes, I will do that as soon as we're done here." Theo nodded.

Julia sighed. "Perhaps I'll take that bottle of water that Ryan offered earlier."

Theo looked at her. "Would you excuse me just a minute?" He went out into the hall along with his employees.

Voices were raised, but the words were muffled by the thick walls. "Sounds like somebody getting in trouble over the bottled water on a platter," Meredith muttered while Julia shook her head.

A few minutes later, Theo returned. He closed the door carefully and returned to his seat. Steepling his hands, the young lawyer seemed to be considering his words carefully.

"I assure you I will get to the bottom of what happened in this conference room."

"It's not that important, Theo," Meredith said. "Really, we didn't think a thing of it."

"No?" He shook his head. "But that's just not done. Why are you excusing it?"

"Because my guess is Ryan is new and hasn't learned not to serve the water in bottles. He'll get the hang of it. Just make sure he's trained to get the nice crystal water pitcher and water glasses. Don't fire him over something so minor."

Theo's face went blank. The room fell into silence.

Then he shook his head. "Wait. I think we're talking about two different things here. Are you saying that Ryan offered you bottled waters on a tray?"

"It was fine, really," Julia said. "That's what we do at our firm." She paused. "Minus the silver tray."

"Although I think maybe we need to have Carmen start using something like that. It does seem a little nicer than just bringing in the water bottles in her hands."

"It does," Julia agreed. "We've got that one pretty tray up in the top of the—"

"Ladies, excuse my interruption, but can we get back to the purpose of our meeting?" Theo paused. "Someone colluded with Stella Fields to have her daughter's DNA tested, and it wasn't me. I assume you know why this happened."

Meredith gave Julia a look. Stella had lied to her.

"We do," Julia said. "Although we thought you were in on the arrangements. Even so, we prefer not to elaborate at this point."

"Nor do you have to," he said. "Pending the results of the tests that Ruth will be setting up, I assume you have a plan for what will happen with Trey Worthington's portion of the inheritance."

"We're working on the details," Julia said, "but yes, we do."

"Is it too early to ask whether you're considering him dead or alive?"

Julia tilted her head. "As I said, we're working on the details, but for the purposes of the list of heirs, we'll be considering him dead."

"I see," came out on a rush of breath. "And you're comfortable with that?"

"We're comfortable that it's the right answer," Julia said. "We're working on securing witnesses and paperwork that will hold up to any challenge that might come along."

Theo nodded. "That is my concern also. And with Trey off the list, his portion is either going to his issue or his heirs at law. Heirs at law would be an equal share to the Worthington twins, unless I miss my guess."

"That's the way I read the statute," Julia said.

"However, I'm at a loss as to how Rose Fields fits in here," Theo said. "She's got a positive DNA test linking her to the Worthingtons. Where does she belong on the chart?"

"That's what a second test will determine," Meredith said smoothly.

"Fair enough. Let's say the test is positive again," Theo said. "Where would you put her on the chart?"

"Equal to the other heirs," Meredith said.

"How?" he pressed. "I fail to see where she fits."

"If the test is positive," Julia said, "then information provided to us by an anonymous source is inaccurate, and Rose Fields is the heir of Trey Worthington's portion of the trust."

"I see." Theo's brows shot up. "Well, that is a surprise."

"It was to us as well," Meredith said. "And that's really all we're at liberty to say at this point. The story is Stella's to tell her daughter, but if she chooses not to, then there will be no other way around it. Rose will have to hear it from us. I have no problem relating that story to her as told to us by our source. Do you, Julia?"

"None at all," Julia said.

"I trust you," Theo said. "So we'll go with your plan."

"Thank you," Julia said. "Just send us a message when you've got the meeting set. We'll keep our schedules clear."

***

That message arrived just before two, when Carmen announced that they had an appointment with Theo Lucas in two hours.

"That Ruth is good," Julia said.

"Now to figure out how to get Sunny there so we can ask her about 1988," Meredith said.

"Do you think she'll be going?"

Meredith grinned. "I might have sent her a text to tell her we were hoping she'd join Kate at the law office when she comes in to speak to Theo because we had something important to discuss with her."

Julia giggled. "You're kidding."

"I'm serious." She showed Julia her phone. "Here's her response."

I HOPE IT'S GOOD NEWS. CAN'T WAIT TO SEE YOU.

Meredith shrugged. "I didn't feel like a response was necessary. Or maybe I should let her know the meeting time?"

"Yes, let her know," Julia agreed.

Meredith texted, MEETING AT FOUR. WILL YOU BE THERE?

It took less than a minute to receive a response. WAS WITH KATE WHEN SHE GOT HER CALL. WILL BE THERE.

"Okay then," Julia said. "Just so we're on the same page with this, how are we going to approach the topic of Trey and a potential offspring and heir?"

"Delicately and with discretion."

"Agreed."

"So we have two hours," Meredith said. "I'm going to see if I can figure out what Trey was alluding to about Sunny." She shrugged. "I guess I'm about to find out."

Chapter Twenty-One

Ruth Felder greeted Meredith and Julia at the door. "Everyone's here," she said in a cheery voice. "We've got the Fields ladies in the Lucas room, the Kate Worthington party in the Wilson room, and Ms. Willadeane Worthington in the Kyler room. Mr. Lucas has offered the use of the Strong conference room should you require a base of operations."

"Thank you," Julia said. "That would be wonderful."

"Follow me, then."

The Strong conference room was a cozier space than Meredith expected. Papered in pale lavender silk with matching drapes drawn away from floor-to-ceiling windows that looked out over a small formal garden and a bubbling fountain, it had the feel of an elegant woman's library rather than a law office conference room.

Instead of a massive table like the one she and Julia had occupied this morning, the focal point of this room featured two curved velvet sofas tufted and covered in the same silk as the drapes. The rug that anchored the room was a lovely Isfahan hand-tied confection of pastels that took Meredith's breath away. She'd fallen in love with a near-twin to this one while planning the decor of her master bedroom but could never have afforded the near six-figure price.

Meredith took a seat on the sofa facing a fireplace where a copy of Monet's painting of water lilies hung in a gold frame. Julia joined her there, placing her notepad and pen on the massive glass coffee table that filled the space between the sofas.

"I would love to own all this luxury," Julia said, "if I could manage to forget the cost of upkeep, insurance, and overhead."

"Ever the practical partner," Meredith said with a grin. "All I see is an idea room in my price-is-no-object she shed."

The pair was still chuckling when the door opened and a man delivered a silver tray containing a crystal pitcher of water, four matching glasses, and a silver ice bucket. Meredith plucked up the folded note emblazoned with the firm's letterhead in their signature navy-blue script.

"Ruth says to let her know who we want to talk to first and she will send them in."

"Forget that," Julia said. "As lovely as this room is, wouldn't you prefer to go to them? They're more relaxed and settled. If we make them come to us, they may tense up again."

"That makes sense. Please let Ruth know we will be conducting our interviews by going to the client," Meredith said to the man. She turned to Julia. "Who first, then?"

"Rose, I think," Julia told her. "That's a conversation I prefer to not delay."

A few minutes later they opened the door to the Lucas conference room to find Rose Fields seated alone at the conference table. The singer—whose face was regularly plastered on magazines, billboards, and of course album covers—sat with her back to the door. Her long legs were encased in faded jeans, and a patchwork kimono wrapped around her shoulders. Sandy hair was captured into two braids that spilled down her back from beneath a brown felt hat.

"Rose?" Meredith said, stepping inside.

She turned around and offered a broad smile. Unlike the face on the billboards and album covers, this one was devoid of makeup and looked ten years younger. "Hey, you're Chase's mom, right?"

"I am, and this is Julia Foley. We would like to talk to you before the test is administered, if you don't mind."

"Sure," she said. "What's up?"

"Where's your mother?" Julia asked.

"Hanging out with Theo, I guess." She shrugged. "Something about telling him a story from the '90s. I wasn't really listening." She pulled a small leather volume of *The Odyssey* from a denim bag. "My road manager told me my reading habits were garbage and I should try one of the classics. Did you know the movie *O Brother, Where Art Thou?* was based on this story? It's blowing my mind."

"I did, actually," Meredith said. "But back to the reason we're here. You're about to take a DNA test. Were you aware that you took one before?"

"My mom told me they tested my water bottle."

"Is that a problem for you?" Julia asked.

"Can't see why it would be."

"And do you have any questions as to why this test is being administered?" Meredith asked.

"Doesn't matter. My mom asks very little of me. She asked me to trust her on this and she would tell me the story after. I figure I'll go along with that."

"You're a good daughter," Julia said. "But are you sure you want to take a test when you don't know the reason for it?"

"I'm not stupid," Rose said. "I've done the math, and I know my mother was pregnant with me when my parents got married. I could get all worked up and figure it has something to do with that, but who cares, you know? I love them. They're my people." She paused. "So can we do it now? The test, I mean."

"Of course." Julia rose and walked to the door then looked outside to catch the attention of a secretary seated at a small desk nearby. "Please tell Theo that Miss Fields is ready for the test."

She stepped back inside, and a few minutes later, Theo returned along with Ruth and a person wearing a lab coat proclaiming him to be Blair Sampson of Linebarger Labs. Blair produced a vial from his kit, labeled and dated it, then instructed Rose how to complete the test.

When she was done, Rose handed the vial back to Blair. He placed a stopper in the vial and gave a nod to Theo. "Let me know when you're ready for the next one."

Meredith handed Rose a business card. "If you have any occasion to wonder what's up, you're an adult and can ask questions. I'll answer them if I'm able."

Rose tucked the card into her book and nodded. "I appreciate that."

"Your mother is in my office," Theo told her. "Please come with me."

After bidding the singer goodbye, Meredith stepped into the hall with Julia behind her. "I think Willadeane should be our next stop, especially considering a text I got from Wally on the way in. I'll explain later."

Julia nodded but said nothing further until they reached the door to the Kyler conference room. "I'm going to let you do the talking," she said. Then she added, "Because of what's happened the last few days."

"Okay." Meredith steeled herself before opening the door. Then she stepped inside. The conference room had been done up in a similar representation of the English country manor that Anson Fields's study had used. Meredith's first reaction was to wonder whether the same decorator had done both rooms.

Then she spied the woman who'd spent part of the weekend in the Savannah jail, now looking fresh and polished, her hair tucked into a French twist and her cheeks pink. She held a twisted handkerchief in her hand.

"Willadeane, are you all right?" were the first words that came to mind, so she said them.

"I'm not," Willadeane admitted. "But I will be. This is just such a shock, and on top of what happened this weekend, I'm just so rattled. I know what I know. What my research shows. And the first test was positive. I just don't understand."

Julia sat next to her and patted her arm. "That's why we're here. To make sense of this and to repeat the test under more controlled circumstances."

Willadeane turned her attention to Julia. "Help me make sense of being arrested on Saturday for an alleged attempt to get more of my supposed inheritance by running down another heir and threatening Mrs. Bellefontaine, and then finding out on Monday I am supposedly not an heir."

"I can't." Julia looked toward Meredith. "But again, we want to have the test repeated."

"Because you think there's an error?"

"Because we want to be certain there isn't," Meredith said. "And as to the events of the weekend, I'm sure all of that will work itself out."

Willadeane opened her mouth as if she might comment and then shook her head. "I would like to do that test now, please."

"I'll let them know," Julia rose and made a quick exit.

Once the door was closed, Willadeane turned her attention to Meredith. "You called the cops on me. Why?"

"No, it wasn't like that at all." She shook her head. "I went down to the police station on Friday to give a witness statement in regard to Kenneth Worthington's whereabouts before the hit-and-run. He had been speaking with me at the park, and I felt the police should know. The detective was aware of my investigation into the Worthington heirs and asked for a list of them with their contact information because he thought there could be a connection." She paused to choose her words carefully. "Witness reports at the scene of the hit-and-run combined with security footage obtained from the Downhome Diner show that Kenneth was hit by a vintage white Cadillac Eldorado."

"I know." Willadeane's shoulders slumped. "There aren't many of those in Savannah."

"Actually," Meredith told her, "according to my data search, there are two. One of them is yours and the other is registered to the Worthingtons."

Willadeane looked down at the tissue she was twisting. "I know. That's why I bought it." She lifted her gaze to meet Meredith's. "I so wanted to be one of them. And not for the wealth, I promise. I found that Eldorado on an online site for less than $5,000. When I went to check it out and sat in it..." She paused. "I felt like I was doing something that my great-grandmother did, and that connection was just priceless. A little part of me didn't feel lost anymore. So I bought it. I guess I sound pretty crazy."

"You don't," Meredith said gently. "Everyone wants to feel like they belong. And I guarantee we all feel lost sometimes." She paused. "I'm sorry about what happened to you on Saturday, but I was only doing what I had to do. I feel terrible that you had to miss out on a spa weekend."

Willadeane smiled. "Actually, that was the part I minded the least. It's one thing for me to take care of someone, and a whole other thing to let someone wait on me. I'm not good at it. And if I had been at that spa on Sunday like I was supposed to be, I would have missed out on being there when Loretta went home to Jesus."

"Loretta?" Meredith asked. "Is she a friend?"

"In a way, though, I'm the only one who remembered that toward the end. She had Alzheimer's. It's a terrible disease, worse when you're alone in the world. I held her hand when she passed, so I can only be thankful about this misunderstanding in regard to the Worthington accident."

Meredith's heart lurched. As much as she wanted to be partial to this woman, she had to maintain a professional distance in her presence.

"Meredith, I was worried when I heard someone had broken in to your home. That's terrifying."

"Thank you." She paused to let out a long breath. "Right before I walked in here earlier, I got a text from a detective at the Savannah PD."

❧ *Chapter Twenty-Two* ❧

MEREDITH CONSIDERED HER WORDS CAREFULLY as she spoke to Willadeane. "The police checked out your car and found there was no damage consistent with it having been in a hit-and-run. They're releasing the vehicle and dropping all charges against you. I'm sure the detective will be calling you once you're out of our meeting today."

Willadeane smiled. "At least something is going right today. I'm very glad to hear this. Thank you for letting me know." She paused. "What about the other one? Did it have damage?"

"The one that belonged to Mrs. Worthington?" At Willadeane's nod, Meredith continued. "No word on that yet."

The door opened, and Julia stepped inside with Blair from the lab following behind. He repeated the instructions he had given to Rose, labeled the vial, and then administered the test.

"Thank you," Willadeane told him when she was done. "How long will I have to wait for these results?"

"The firm is paying for expedited results, so Mr. Lucas and Magnolia Investigations will have a copy in their inboxes tomorrow morning."

"That's very good news. Is there anything else I need to do here?"

"Nothing else," Julia told her. "We'll be in touch as soon as we have something to tell you."

Willadeane rose and said her goodbyes then headed out the door. Once she was gone, Meredith shook her head. "I have never met someone so thankful, Julia. I really like her."

"I like her too," Julia said. "We'll just have to see what happens tomorrow."

Meredith let out a long breath. "Okay, it's time for Kate. I have an idea. What if you supervise Kate's test and I speak with Sunny?"

"Divide and conquer," Julia said. "I like it. But are you sure you want to take on that conversation with Sunny alone? Sometimes it is good to have two sets of ears listening rather than just one. We all remember things slightly differently."

"I suppose you're right. But I don't want to talk to Sunny with her daughter present."

"Agreed."

Julia knocked once then stepped into the Wilson conference room. The disheveled Sunny was nowhere in sight. The woman who looked up from her phone and smiled when they walked in was as camera ready as any photo shoot model.

She wore the same shade of pink as the pajamas she'd worn at the lake, but this time it was in the form of a velour tracksuit with white stripes bearing a designer's name down the arms of the jacket and the legs of the pants. The effect was elegant vacation casual, and the colors set off the deep tan Sunny had acquired in the short time since Meredith had seen her.

Kate wore full stage makeup, and her hair had been tamed into a take-me-seriously style with the application of copious amounts of hair spray. In contrast to her mother, Kate barely acknowledged them as she talked into a gold phone that had been slipped between her cheek and her lacquered blond hair.

Sunny jumped up to hug Meredith. "It's so good to see you," she said.

"You as well." Meredith stepped back so the team that had followed her in could get into position. "Twice in just a few days. That's more than we've seen one another in the last six months."

"It might have been three times, but I had to miss the Junior League tennis tournament on Saturday." Her pink painted lips turned up into a grin. "I heard your friend Larry took the trophy. I hope he realizes he will have to come back next year and defend his title."

Meredith stifled a smile at the thought of how "Larry" would react when he heard the news. "That will depend on whether he's in town, I suppose."

Kate moved the phone from her ear. "Let's get this over with, please. My decorator is being impossible, and I can just imagine this call will go on for a while."

Once again they watched as Blair completed the process of administering the DNA test. Then he returned the labeled vial to its place alongside the others that had been collected and made his exit.

Kate picked up her phone and resumed her conversation while Meredith focused on Sunny. "I would prefer to talk to you somewhere else. Do you mind?"

"No, of course not." She looked over at Kate. "Mummy is going to go talk to Julia and Meredith."

Her daughter waved her hand to dismiss them all without missing a beat in her conversation. "Okay then," Sunny said. "After you."

A few minutes later they were situated in the Strong room with Julia and Meredith seated together and Sunny across from them. "This is such a pretty room. I'm going to have to take pictures before I leave. I might steal some of these ideas for the condo in Florida."

"So, Sunny," Meredith began, ignoring the statement, "has Kenneth been located?"

"There's no news," she told them. "Chip is being closemouthed about it, so I suspect they've talked, but nobody is telling me anything." She paused. "I did hear that the lady they arrested was released."

"She didn't do it," Meredith said.

"There was no damage on her vehicle consistent with an accident of that type," Julia added. "You said Chip is being closemouthed. Is he worried about Kenneth at all?"

"He's always worried about Kenneth for one reason or another. So the general answer is of course. Specific to his current situation? I'm not sure." She paused. "Do you know who did this room? I have got to find him or her. It's just stunning."

"I do not," Meredith said. "And as to our children, you never stop having concerns about them, even when they're grown. At least I don't."

"It's fascinating how they took Monet's masterpiece and shrunk it to fit the space." Sunny rose and walked over to the painting to inspect it. "This gives me so many ideas. I mean, really. I can just see a shrunken version of the Mona Lisa in our dining room in the city."

"The Mona Lisa is already quite small," Julia offered.

Meredith could tell her partner was struggling not to roll her eyes. Time to try again to redirect Sunny's attention.

"Sunny, we have a message for you from Trey."

She froze, her back still to them. Then, slowly she turned around, her face white.

"Say that again," came out as a rough whisper.

"We have a message for you," Meredith repeated.

"Trey wants his share of the money, doesn't he?" she spat out in a tone that sounded nothing like the Sunny Conrad Meredith knew. "It figures he would return from the grave and face the Mob in order to get his greedy hands on my children's inheritance."

"Your children will still get their inheritance as long as they meet the qualifications," Julia reminded her.

"Which they, of course, do. But it will be divided by three, not two." Sunny exhaled sharply. "No, by four. That woman who…" She shook her head. "No, even if she didn't try to run my son down in broad daylight, she's a crackpot. She is definitely not a Worthington."

"Sit down, Sunny," Julia said in that calm but assertive voice she must have used a thousand times in the courtroom.

The demand worked. Sunny sank onto the plush purple sofa and leaned her head back. For a minute, Meredith wasn't sure if she would speak again.

Then Sunny sat up abruptly. "Do I get to know where he is?"

"No," Julia told her.

"What about how to find him? As in to get a message to him? They obviously do that or you wouldn't have found him. Or did he find you?" She paused. "Sure, of course. He found you because he didn't want to miss out on any of Granny's money."

"We cannot speak to any of that, Sunny," Meredith said. "Nor can we share any of the details of how this conversation came about."

"But he is alive, right? I mean he would have to be in order to send a message."

"He was at some point." This from Julia, who looked pleased with herself for skirting the specifics.

"Past tense?" Sunny asked, watching Julia closely.

"No comment," she responded.

"Okay, moving on. Would you like to hear the message from Trey?" Meredith asked.

Sunny shrugged as if she didn't care, but the expression on her face betrayed her. "Sure."

Meredith paused. "He said to tell you, 'Gotcha.'"

Sunny sat very still. She barely blinked. Her hands rested on her knees, and her eyes were focused somewhere behind them.

"Gotcha," Sunny repeated, shaking her head.

"Yes," Julia told her. "He was very specific."

Sunny leaned forward, bejeweled fingers drumming a cadence on her knees. "What else did he tell you?"

"That was his only message to you," Meredith said. "Do you know what it means?"

"Oh, of course I do." Sunny rose and collected her vintage red Chanel purse. "It means I'm very glad he's decided to remain dead. Dead to me, regardless."

"Wait," Meredith called as Sunny stalked toward the door. "I want to talk about what happened in 1988."

The door slammed. Sunny was gone.

Julia gave Meredith a sideways glance, her brows raised. "So, what do you suppose happened in 1988?"

Meredith shrugged. "I have no clue."

"Sunny seems to think you know something," Julia said.

"I know." Meredith grinned "It'll be interesting to see what she does with the information."

"I'm a little concerned about that, Meredith. If Trey was holding something awful over her head and she thinks we know about it, who knows what she'll do."

"Oh, come on," Meredith said, laughing. "This is Sunny Conrad we're talking about. She wouldn't dare do anything that would jeopardize her bid for president of the local chapter of the Daughters of the American Revolution."

"The question is, what will she do if someone has information that might keep her from that goal? I have a bad feeling about her, Meredith." Julia paused. "I've never been a mother, but was it odd to you that she was so calm about her son's disappearance? Wouldn't you be frantic if one of your boys had been the victim of a hit-and-run and then gone this long without letting you know he's all right?"

"Okay, you're right. That is a bit suspicious."

Julia snatched up her purse. "I guess all we can do now is wait for the DNA results."

Meredith's phone buzzed with a text from Wally. WORTHINGTON CADILLAC IS MIA.

She pressed the call button, and Wally answered immediately. "I figured you'd want more information than that," the detective said with a chuckle.

"Who owns that car, exactly? And by that, I mean which family member?"

"Not a family member," he said. "It's owned by Mrs. Worthington's trust."

"Which means the Worthington heirs own it," she said. "But who has access?"

"Apparently, anyone in the family who can find it, start it, and drive it." Wally paused. "Sorry, but when you're talking about use of an automobile, the sky's the limit. We have to find out where it was, where it is, and how it got between the two places."

"Any luck on the security cameras at the scene?"

"Nothing of any value. The driver was wearing a hoodie, and the face is obscured."

"Remind me, Wally. Which way was that car heading?"

"North, toward the park," he said. "Why?"

"No reason. I'm just trying to piece something together." She let out a long breath. "Will you let me know if you find out more? I'm curious."

"Will do." He paused. "And Meredith, just so you know, we still have no idea who put that envelope in your kitchen. I'm sorry I don't have more to report on that."

"I know you're working on it," she said. "And thank you for understanding that I don't need a babysitter."

"I'm doing that under protest."

She tucked the phone into her purse and found Julia watching her. "Why are you looking at me like that?"

"I'm still not sure you should have refused the offer of an officer shadowing you."

"I changed the locks. I have a weapon and am trained to use it." She shrugged. "I'll be fine."

"I have to admit right now I'm more worried about Sunny than anyone else. She wasn't happy with you. With either of us."

Chapter Twenty-Three

Wilhelmina Worthington walked into the lobby of the Styles National Bank like she owned the place. Not because she did, but Daddy had, so that was close enough.

Six years ago she'd taken home from Theo's office an envelope from her late husband. The first two weeks after she'd dropped that envelope into her handbag, she'd had no desire to touch it. Then she became curious.

The idea that there might be a pile of cash in there occurred to her, but she quickly set that foolishness aside. Daniel had made his point by leaving her one dollar. Daniel would never ruin that statement by adding to the amount.

Then the doctor pronounced her the proud owner of a terminal case of cancer and declared she would die within the year. Wilhelmina told him she had no time to concern herself with that sort of nonsense. Then she'd gone on to live her life as if she'd never heard the words.

She had outlived that doctor, but this new one seemed to have a little clearer grasp of the actual timetable for her demise. So far every one of his predictions in regard to her health had come true.

So when he told her she had less than two weeks, Wilhelmina knew he expected her to draw her family together and lean on their loving arms until she expired.

Rubbish.

She would do no such thing.

Instead, Wilhelmina drove to her grandson Tommy Two's home and left her car in his garage. Then she had her almost-granddaughter, Sunny, take her home.

She and Sunny had gotten along famously since the first day Spencer brought Sunny home four years ago when they met in sophomore history class. Sunny quickly became the granddaughter she'd never had. Wilhelmina saw immediately that the relationship between her grandson and Sunny was "just friends," but she had hoped they would change that. Even though she and Sunny shared no blood relation, they were two of a kind. Though Wilhelmina knew that would be a burden to carry in Sunny's later years, she wouldn't dare give her a hint of the challenges to come.

Better to be young and looking ahead knowing anything was possible than to be seventy-seven years old and warning someone what might happen. She knew all too well that fierce love was costly.

And painful.

And that Sunny Worthington loved with a fierceness that would take her far and someday cause her to do something she would regret.

Even though it would be in the name of love.

Sunny had driven her out to Tybee Island, to the little fishing cottage that no one in the family knew about. Once there, Wilhelmina told her this little piece of paradise, humble as it was, was now hers and she was to keep that fact to herself.

Then she had Sunny drive her to the law office in her zippy white Mustang convertible with the top down and their scarves and sunglasses in place so Wilhelmina could sign the deed to make that happen. With that piece of business, almost everything she wanted to do was done.

There was just one more task to complete.

Wilhelmina grasped the brass handrail that had been put in when Daddy got too old to take these stairs two at a time. He'd situated the lobby of the Styles National Bank on the second floor because he claimed it made for a grand two-story entrance and a lovely view out of the upper lobby.

She knew better though. Daddy just wanted to spend his days looking down on the good folks of Savannah, a sentiment she understood even if she didn't feel that way herself.

She'd had to give up her Chanel pumps three years ago when her podiatrist told her he'd fire her as a client if she didn't start wearing more sensible shoes. Sunny had been the recipient of those too. She'd kept the purses but tucked a note in the special ones to see that they went to Sunny when she was gone.

At least Chanel hadn't stopped making dresses she liked. She'd chosen red today, in honor of the occasion. It seemed only fitting.

Wilhelmina touched the pearls at her neck. The Worthington pearls, as they were known now, though Daddy had named them the Styles Cotillion pearls way back when he gave them to her to wear as a debutante at the 1917 Christmas Cotillion.

The set contained a necklace of perfectly matched eight-millimeter pearls that had been hand-tied in some remote village in Japan way back before the turn of the century, and a pair of earrings that she'd recently had converted from clip to pierced. The pearls had been the envy of the other debs and her pride and joy, at least until Thomas came along and she realized that people were far more important than things.

Oh, but those pearl earrings.

Wilhelmina chuckled as she arrived at the top step, even as she gave thanks for a sturdy rail and her own perseverance. Her doctor hadn't been too happy about her getting her ears pierced at the age of seventy-six. While he complained of the risks, she ignored him. She'd never tell him it hurt like the dickens and she wished she hadn't done it.

Daddy would have called that a good opportunity to keep her mouth shut. And so she did.

Then she called Sunny to come get those pearls too.

"Mrs. Worthington!"

Wilhelmina cringed. The last thing she wanted was to be spotted.

And yet she apparently had attracted the attention of the bank's current president. She allowed him to catch up to her, and then she managed a smile.

"Good morning, Percy."

She remembered Percy Kimble when he scrambled around his daddy's Texaco station making sure the tires of the Eldorado were aired up just right. Now here he was in a brown three-piece polyester suit with one of those loud wide ties that were in fashion right now.

If she was of a mind to speak the truth, Wilhelmina would have told him she liked him better in those baggy green coveralls with the red star on the pocket. Back then he did honest work. Right now he looked like he was about to try and sell her a swayback mare for twice what it was worth.

"How can I help you today?" he asked her.

Wilhelmina opened her right fist to reveal a safe deposit key. She'd been clutching it ever since her chauffeur helped her into the back seat of the big black Lincoln that Tommy insisted she be driven around town in.

She handed it over to Percy without comment.

"Let me get you over to the vault. It's right over—"

"I know where it is," she snapped. "I was playing hide-and-seek in there before I knew how to spell my name."

She hadn't. Not here. She was thinking of the old bank building. The smaller one that Daddy had sold to the law firm after he built his grand banking palace, as he called it.

"Just open the box and leave it for me to look through. I won't require any assistance beyond that."

He looked as if he might argue. Then he thought better of it.

"Yes, ma'am."

Off he went strutting through the lobby, dipping his head to this one and that until he disappeared into the vault. Wilhelmina continued her walk in that direction, ignoring the same important people Percy had just greeted.

She'd never liked most of them and didn't care to pretend. The rest would know she was busy and had no inclination toward small talk even when she wasn't.

Percy found her waiting for him when he emerged from the vault. "I've taken the liberty of putting you in a room with a chair so you'll be comfortable. Would you like me to bring you something to drink? Water or iced tea?"

"Nothing, thank you." She allowed him to settle her in a viewing room—at least that's what Daddy called them, though she always thought it sounded like something related to a funeral—and then sat very still until he finally stopped making a pest of himself and went away.

Only then did Wilhelmina make her way to the door and turn the bolt in the lock. There would be no interruptions now. Not until she pressed the buzzer that would alert a bank clerk she was ready to have the box put away again.

Nothing to keep her from finally facing whatever it was Daniel left behind for her to find.

Her hands trembled on a good day, but today they could barely lift the lid on the ancient box. When the bank was renovated, they'd left the boxes as Daddy's carpenter had built them. Thus, the wood in her hands had been put in place almost one hundred years before by a man who was trained in Germany and laid to rest in the Bonaventure Cemetery when it was barely a weed patch with a few headstones.

Or at least that was her recollection of the old man's funeral.

Daddy had been partial to that old carpenter. So partial that he'd had the old man move all the safe-deposit boxes to the new building and fit them into the new vault. It was disconcerting to recall this room in two different buildings, but that was what happened when one lived so very long. Memories swirled and settled, and everything wasn't always where you left it.

Or where it should be.

Wilhelmina fumbled with the latch and finally lifted the lid. The smell of dust and memories rose thick and sure, stinging her vision.

No, she would not cry. Not yet.

And maybe not ever.

There were only two things in the box. One was a paper-wrapped package addressed to a Deanie Worthington at Wilhelmina's address. There was no postage on the package nor was there a return address.

She set it aside and reached for the envelope. It was brown and slightly larger than a postal envelope. Written in Daniel's atrocious handwriting was a single word: WILLA.

She turned it over and unwrapped the string that held the envelope closed and then upended it to find there were two more envelopes inside. She opened the smaller of the pair, a pale pink envelope that looked like it might contain a greeting card.

Ignoring decorum in favor of speed, she ripped the sealed envelope open and pulled out a folded piece of paper. Wilhelmina recognized the paper at once as having come from the stationery she kept Daniel supplied with at his desk, both at home and at the office.

Rather than read whatever Daniel had written, she postponed the moment by returning to the paper-wrapped package. Tearing into it, she pulled the paper away to see a folded piece of yellowed fabric and a crudely made cloth doll wearing a little pink dress.

Wilhelmina ran her hand over the cloth and tried to make sense of what this was. What it meant.

The tremors sent the pile of fabric tumbling to the floor where it puddled around her chair and the sensible shoes she'd selected for today's jaunt into town. With great difficulty, Wilhelmina managed to maneuver herself off the chair and within reach of the fabric.

Straightening with the cloth between her thumbs and forefingers, Wilhelmina's breath caught. She swayed.

It was the Worthington christening gown.

Her fingers clumsily arranged the fabric on the table. Someone had added some trim to the collar. Lace, it was. At the edges of the sleeves too. They'd sewed in a neat row of tiny white pearl buttons down the front.

Where it had been a dignified family piece fit for a boy—her boys—under an unknown seamstress's gifted hand, it had become a beautiful gown to present a little girl to the church.

So many questions. Who had done this and why? Where had it come from? Why had Daniel thought to leave it here for her to find?

She retrieved the other envelope, the creamy white rectangle with no markings, and turned it over. Unlike the other ones, this one was not sealed, so the contents fell out easily when she pulled at them.

A birth certificate.

An adoption certificate.

Wilhelmina frowned. What was all of this? It certainly did not pertain to Simon. When he joined the family it was done quietly without a paper trail to follow back to the parents who did not want to be found.

Or in this case, the guilty parties who did not want to be shunned by polite society.

Her eyes weren't as good as they used to be, so the tiny print on the birth certificate presented a problem. By squinting she could read the first line:

BABY GIRL WORTHINGTON

And the mother's name:

Deanie Phillips, Vancouver, Canada

And finally, the father's name:

Benjamin Daniel Worthington, PFC USMC Deceased

Wilhelmina's tears fell now in earnest. So there had been a baby. Daniel had told her those were lies. That this woman who'd wanted to be part of the family did not have a child that carried the Worthington name. That she was after money, so he gave it to her and sent her away.

And yet here it was.

Proof of yet another lie Daniel had told her.

At least in part.

Reluctantly, she set the birth certificate aside and reached for the adoption certificate. "Charleston Home for Unwed Mothers," she whispered. "Daniel, you sly dog. No wonder you gave ridiculously large donations to that charity. They were keeping your secret, and you were paying them for their discretion. Again."

She let out a long breath, dabbing her eyes with a handkerchief before attempting to read the papers. For there wasn't just a certificate. Other papers had been stapled together.

It took quite some time, but Wilhelmina managed to read every word on those pages. Then she sat back to let it all sink in.

It had been about the money all along. Daniel had spent his entire life buying everything he wanted. The only purchase he hadn't been able to make was her.

Wilhelmina couldn't be bought. That irked him so.

She let out a shuddering breath. The pain was a noiseless shout now, reminding her that the clock the doctor set in motion was ticking swiftly and loudly.

From the birth certificate to the adoption certificate, the paper trail of payments spelled out the truth of what had been done right under her nose. Sweet Ben—the gentle man whose inability to allow Daniel to buy his way out of a war that led to his death—had been a husband and a father.

Somewhere out there was a little girl, Baby Girl Worthington, who had been bought and paid for by a man who hadn't asked her if she might want him to do it.

Worse, the mother of this little girl had gone along with whatever offer Daniel had made. She'd been taken in by the prospect of riches—because Daniel would have paid her well—and this child had been the one to suffer the loss of not only her mother but also her father.

Wilhelmina dipped her head, her eyes once again filling. "Lord, wherever that child is right now, would You favor her with the Worthington name someday? I'm too old to find her, but You're beyond all time and age. And if it isn't too much to ask, would You see that she gets everything? This little baby girl, she's going to need something more. If I could, I would give it to her. I can't, but You can."

She said a soft amen.

It was time.

Wilhelmina reached over to take up the folded page of Daniel's stationery. Then, eyes closed, she flattened the paper in front of her.

Though she intended to pray again, no words came. So she opened her eyes and saw what she never thought she would ever see.

An apology from Daniel Worthington.

I couldn't bring myself to say it when I was alive, but I will say it now. I'm sorry, Willa, for all the wrong I've done to you and this family, and there has been much. I have no defense other than much of what I did, I did because I thought it was the right thing at the time.

I was wrong. Please forgive me.

In my own way, I loved you most though I showed it so poorly. I was always in awe of you. Always trying to prove I was worthy of you. Turns out I never was. Daniel

Wilhelmina took great care in putting everything back how she found it. Seven days later, she returned and added the letter she'd painstakingly written over the last week then closed the box, drew back the bolt to unlock the door, and pressed the buzzer.

Percy saw that she was returned safely to the Lincoln, where her driver fussed over her until she finally hushed him up. "I want to see Theo Lucas. Take me there now."

It was a pitifully short drive, nothing she couldn't have managed in under five minutes at a snail's pace a few years ago. He pulled up out front, and she had the oddest desire to go around back and break in.

But she was beyond that now. A pity.

Theo came immediately, as she knew he would. Wilhelmina lowered the window and stretched out her hand then dropped the key into his palm.

"Put this in my trust," she told him.

"But it's a key," Theo protested.

"I can see that. Just keep it safe and give it to my heirs." She paused. "Or heir, perhaps, if I get my way."

"Of course."

"Make sure that there's a note with that key, since you won't live forever." At his grin, she continued. "I wrote a letter. I know what you did in helping Daniel see that Ben's daughter was adopted. I won't ask you to tell me where she is. I don't have that kind of time left. But I want you to promise that when she's found—and I know the Lord is going to see that happen—that she knows there's something in that box just for her from me."

"For Ben's daughter," he said. "And not for Tommy Two's offspring?"

She waved away the question with a sweep of her hand. "Yes, for Ben's daughter. Now promise it, Theo. I need to hear it."

"I promise, Willa."

Then she raised the tinted window and ordered the driver to go, knowing she would never see dear Theo again this side of heaven.

And knowing that everything would be fine all the same.

Chapter Twenty-Four

MEREDITH WAITED TO CHECK HER emails until Julia was there too. Thus she paced her office until finally the back door opened.

"In here," she called, and Julia's footsteps headed her direction. "The email is in my inbox. Yours too, I would guess."

"I don't know," Julia said. "I was afraid to look. Go ahead and open it now."

Meredith opened the email from Blair then groaned. "It has an attachment I have to click on. Hold on."

The attachment opened with maddening slowness. "Of all the times for the internet to be dragging," Julia complained.

"Wait, here we go."

Meredith watched the list populate. One by one the names appeared.

KATE COLLINS—HEIR

ROSE FIELDS—NOT HEIR

WILLADEANE WORTHINGTON—HEIR

Meredith sat back and stared at the results. "Julia, she was telling the truth."

"And so was Trey," she added.

"Okay," Meredith said. "I'm going to call Theo to see if he's opened his email."

Before she could dial his number, her phone rang. "I assume you've read the results," Theo said.

"Yes, Julia and I just did. As agreed, since Kate is a match, so is Kenneth. That gives us three heirs with Trey's portion going back into the pot to be split among them."

"You're certain," he said.

"Theo," Julia said. "Are you trying to worry us?"

He chuckled. "No, just doing my due diligence and making sure you've qualified everyone based on DNA as well as the legitimacy of their parents' marriage at their birth. Of course I know you have, but I'll wait for the formal report from you before we go any further on planning our distributions from the trust."

"Yes, absolutely," Meredith said, frowning.

"What's wrong?" Julia asked once they'd hung up with Theo. "I saw your expression change. That always means you're thinking about something."

"It's probably nothing. Very likely out of the scope of our investigation into the heirs."

"And yet?" Julia gave her a sideways look. "Let's hear it."

"I never did actually print out the paperwork verifying Sunny's marriage to Spencer Worthington. It's a little thing, but it bugs me that I skipped that step. And it's one that will have to be done before we can file an official report."

"Especially after the message Trey sent Sunny?" Julia offered.

"Exactly." Meredith reduced her mail program and opened the public data search that she used in investigations. "I'll just print off their marriage license and be done with it."

"Whatever makes you feel okay with the results," Julia said. "We'll need to let the heirs know. I'm sure they're all sitting by their phones."

"Why don't you make the calls to Willadeane and Rose? Do you mind?" She typed in the password, and the investigative program began to load. "By the time you're done giving them the news, I'll have what I need and we can put the report together."

"Absolutely," Julia said. "I think I'll just tell Rose that the report showed no relation and leave it at that. If she wants to know more, she can ask Theo or her mama."

"I doubt she will. Remember, she wasn't too curious anyway."

"No, it was Stella who was behind it all, and she likely has some answering to do to Theo regarding how she manipulated the first test. I'm assuming it has something to do with why Theo had words with that intern, Ryan." Julia rose and headed back toward her office.

Meredith typed in the search words she needed in order to find the marriage license for Spencer and Sunny's 1989 wedding. Then she waited for the results.

And sat back gaping when she found them.

"Julia," she shouted, despite the fact her partner just might be on the phone. "Julia!"

A moment later, Julia came running, her phone in her hand. "I'm so sorry, Rose," she said. "I thought there was an emergency."

"There is," Meredith said.

"I'm going to have to hang up now," Julia said. "Remember, if you have any questions about your result, please call Theo Lucas at the law firm." She hung up and frowned. "What in the world is wrong with you, Meredith? You knew I would be on the phone. I haven't even had a chance to call Willadeane yet."

"Good, because the situation has changed." She hit PRINT on the records page and then navigated to the documents that needed to be printed. "Give me a second and I'll show you."

Julia sat down and placed her phone on the desk. A moment later, Meredith placed three pages in front of her.

"Okay, here's what I found. This is in chronological order. The first one is a marriage license between Sunny Worthington and some guy named William Nolan, whose employment is listed as musician. The date is June 1988."

Julia lifted the page and studied it then looked back up at Meredith. "She was married before Spencer?"

"A year before. That's what she was doing in 1988 that Trey was referring to." She paused. "Well, that was part of it. Check this out." Meredith handed her the second page she'd printed. "That is a marriage license between Sunny and Spencer Worthington, dated August 1989. Spencer died in October of 1991, leaving her a widow. Then comes the marriage to Chip in 1993. This is the supposed second wedding between the widow and the financier that made the papers and obviously is still ongoing. But look at this." She handed Julia the third document, which was several pages long. "Don't miss the date on that one."

"It's a divorce decree. The parties are Sunny Nolan and William Nolan." Julia thumbed through to the last page then looked up at Meredith in disbelief. She shook her head. "It's dated January 1991." Julia let the papers fall back onto the desk. "Sunny was a bigamist. Her marriage to William Nolan didn't end until two years after she married Spencer."

"And one year after the twins were born. So she wouldn't have been lawfully married to Spencer at the time—a specific stipulation in the will."

"*Gotcha*," Julia said.

Meredith picked up her phone and called Sunny's number then placed the call on SPEAKER so Julia could listen in. She had no idea whether the woman was an early riser or not but felt certain she would be awake this morning.

Sunny picked up on the second ring. "Tell me you've got good news, Meredith," she said cheerily.

"I'm calling regarding the naming of the heirs," Meredith told her. "The results have come in, and Kate's been matched as an heir, thus Kenneth would likely be considered one as well, assuming we can locate him and verify he is still alive."

"Of course," Sunny replied. "When will the funds be divided and distributed?"

"Theo would have to answer that." She paused to give Julia a look. "But first, I have a question for you."

"Sure, anything," Sunny said.

"Does the name William Nolan mean anything to you?"

Silence.

"Sunny?"

"I'm here," she said, her voice strained.

"Sunny, our records search turned up evidence that you were a bigamist."

"I, well…" Her words stopped. "Theo fixed that. It was a stupid mistake. Will told me he'd had our marriage annulled. I believed him. My parents had no idea I'd even married him, so it wasn't like

I could go to them for help. I had no idea until Spencer looked into it after the twins were born. Funny, but I don't even remember why."

"I'm sure he was surprised."

"No," she said. "He was mortified. He said I had broken the law and was in danger of being arrested if something wasn't done immediately. I was breastfeeding twins and trying to figure out how to get more than four hours of sleep in a night, so you can imagine I wasn't much help to him in fixing that stupid mistake. But Theo was. One day he sent over papers and I signed them, and that was that."

"Yes," Meredith said. "That was that. Until now."

"What do you mean?"

"The terms of the will require that the parents of the heir be legally married at the time of their birth. You and Spencer Worthington were not legally married at the time of the twins' birth."

"So the twins don't inherit?" Sunny asked slowly. "They get nothing from Granny?"

"I'm sorry." Meredith paused. "I wish I had better news."

Sunny laughed. "Oh, Meredith, you don't understand. This is absolutely the best news I've heard all day."

"Sunny?" Meredith said. "Maybe you didn't hear me correctly. Both of your children just lost out on one third of a large inheritance. How can that possibly be a good day?"

She sighed. "Okay, Meredith, this is between us."

"Then I need to disclose that Julia is here with me listening," she said.

"No problem. So here's the deal. Right now Kenneth is hiding out at the Tybee Island house that used to belong to Granny. It's a place only a few people know about. Even Chip doesn't know, although he'll be finding out today."

"Why is he hiding?" Julia asked.

"It all has to do with money and high-interest loans. Kenneth got in over his head going around the country presenting *Skate with Skate* shows on a small budget. Chip and I offered to put money into the business, but he was too stubborn to allow it. Apparently he had a show last Saturday that might have put him in the black, but a shady character he had some dealings with in Charleston got wind of the event and showed up last week demanding his money. He made threats. Said he would take out his revenge on the skaters. That was too much for my son. He wasn't about to risk harm to the kids. So Kenneth decided to disappear until he could figure out what to do."

"And by disappear, you mean have someone drive Wilhelmina's Eldorado in a fake hit-and-run?"

"It had to be something dramatic, or that awful man would never believe it. The word was out that Kenny was about to come into a large amount of money. The guy wasn't going to be left out of that payday. So being hit by a car is a pretty good reason to cancel a skating event and buy time."

"Who was driving the car, Sunny? Was it you?"

"No! I could never do that. Kenneth had one of his friends from the skate park do it."

"Will the police be pressing charges against either one of them?" Julia asked.

"No, they're more interested in the guy who threatened him and the kids than they are in Kenneth or his friend at this point.

And it'll be another relief to Kenny that he's not inheriting, since he turns his back on all the trappings of wealth unless we force money on him."

"What about Kate?" Julia asked. "How will she take this?"

"I don't know if she mentioned it to you, but I always downplayed the Worthington trust to the twins. Trey was all about the money he would be splitting with them. It was obnoxious. I would tell them there wasn't that much there and that they probably wouldn't inherit anyway. I guess maybe that was preparing them for today. I'm not sorry I did it. And since Kate wasn't looking for anything, she won't be disappointed much when she doesn't get it."

"I hope that's right," Meredith said. "That's a big payday to be bypassed on."

"Kate will be fine, and so will Kenneth." Sunny paused. "Oh, and one more thing," she said. "That break-in at your place? We're pretty sure it must have been the same man who was after Kenneth who was behind that. He wanted his money, and since you and Julia were naming heirs, I guess he thought he could hurry up the process."

"Have you told this to the police?"

"Not yet," she said.

"I'm going to text you a number for my friend Wally Parker at the Savannah PD. Call him and tell him what you've told me. He'll handle everything."

"Thank you, Meredith," Sunny said. "I will."

Meredith hung up and shook her head. "None of that happened like I expected."

"And yet it fits all the pieces nicely into place, doesn't it?" Julia asked.

"All but one." She picked up her phone, put it on SPEAKER, and dialed.

"Willadeane," she said when the phone was answered. "I've got some news for you."

"Oh," Willadeane said. "I'm going to need to call you back. I'm in the middle of a bath."

"Did we catch you in the tub?" Julia asked.

"No, one of my Alzheimer ladies," she told her. "Much as I've been waiting to hear this news, I need to give my full attention to her. She's the most important thing right now."

Meredith bid her goodbye then hung up the phone. "That lady just inherited a hundred million dollars and a family. She's been fighting to be recognized by them for more than ten years, and yet, at this moment, she is bathing a woman who won't remember who she is the next time she sees her."

Julia smiled. "There are still good people in the world."

"And the Lord still blesses them."

Dear Reader,

When I began the task of planning the direction of Meredith Bellefontaine and Julia Foley's next adventures as the proprietors of Magnolia Investigations, I was fairly certain I wanted to write a story set in the legal field. You see, on the days when I'm not wearing my writing hat, I am a certified probate and family law paralegal and a proud member of the Texas Bar Association's Paralegal Division.

What I didn't realize was that I would not only be using my legal knowledge to weave a behind-the-scenes tale of what goes on in the probate process, but I would also be reminding myself of what is most important in life. Like the matriarch of the Worthington clan, Wilhelmina Styles Worthington, I learned that no matter how hard I try to make life less messy, people are human and, in the end, what we leave behind as far as our legacy is so much more important than any pile of money we leave in a bank account.

Last year I learned firsthand how very short life can be and how very abrupt and unexpected is the day a loved one can be called home. I urge you to love your people while they are here. Ignore their faults and just love them.

Be a Willadeane and focus on what is important in the moment. I promise if you do, God will take care of the rest.

Enjoy!

Signed,
Kathleen Y'Barbo

About the Author

BESTSELLING AUTHOR KATHLEEN Y'BARBO IS a multiple Carol Award and RITA nominee and bestselling author of more than one hundred books with over two million copies of her books in print in the US and abroad. A tenth-generation Texan and certified paralegal, she is a member of the Texas Bar Association Paralegal Division, Texas A&M Association of Former Students, and the Texas A&M Women Former Students (Aggie Women), Texas Historical Society, Novelists Inc., and American Christian Fiction Writers. She would also be a member of the Daughters of the American Republic, Daughters of the Republic of Texas, and a few others if she would just remember to fill out the paperwork that Great-Aunt Mary Beth has sent her more than once.

When she's not spinning modern-day tales about her wacky Southern relatives, Kathleen inserts an ancestor or two into her historical and mystery stories as well. She also writes (mostly) relative-free cozy mystery novels for Guideposts Books.

Kathleen and her hero-in-combat-boots husband have their own surprise love story that unfolded on social media a few years back. They make their home just north of Houston, Texas, and are the parents and in-laws of a blended family of Texans, Okies, and one very adorable Londoner.

To find out more about Kathleen or connect with her through social media, check out her website at kathleenybarbo.com.

An Armchair Tour of Savannah

The Skate Park

SAVANNAH'S PARKS ARE LEGENDARY. HOME to the famous fountains that grace the city, parks were incorporated into the city's planning from the beginning. However, it was not until recently that skate parks were added as a feature. As a mother to two sons who spent countless hours on skateboards and rollerblades, I am thrilled to showcase a fictionalized version of this park in this book.

In my story, the fictional Kenneth "Skate" Worthington frequents a skate park which, for convenience's sake, I situated near the also fictional Downhome Diner. Thanks to a volunteer group known as the Chatham County Skate Park Supporters (CCSPS), however, there is a real skate park located in Lake Meyer Park.

Skating on the streets is dangerous at best, and in some places within the city either illegal or strongly discouraged. Worse, people make assumptions about people on skateboards that are often derogatory, and sometimes they act on those assumptions. All of this adds up to a less-than-stellar environment for kids and adults to practice a sport that takes skill, attention to detail, and a massive amount of guts. (Can you tell I am a skate mom?)

Thus, for far too long skaters in Savannah faced the dilemma of where to go to enjoy their sport. From this, a grassroots effort spear-headed by the CCSPS—made up of skaters and parents of skaters—set into motion the slow-moving process of providing a safe environ-ment for skaters. The end goal was to build a park that would challenge the skaters while keeping them off the streets and out of danger.

In 2009, CCSPS began working with the county Public Works and Parks and Recreation department to find a space that would work for skaters who were, until then, having to go out of state to find a park where they could safely skate. Thanks in part to a T-shirt campaign with Marc Jacobs International, a grant from the Tony Hawk Foundation, and a massive local campaign, their dream of a local skate park became a reality. Local fundraising efforts con-tinue, as witnessed by the many opportunities to help listed on the skate park's website, savannahskatepark.com.

Kudos to Savannah and CCSPS! Check out their website for more information on the park and its events, and to have a look at the folks behind the effort. Their illustrious ranks include teachers, accountants, artists, musicians, a city council member, and more than one proud parent of a skater.

One more caveat: next time you see someone on a skateboard, think of the list of skaters shown on the savannahskate.com website and realize there is more to him or her than baggy pants and a hoodie on wheels. And if your city doesn't have a skate park, per-haps it should. Just ask the folks in Savannah!

SOMETHING DELICIOUS FROM A
Downhome Southern Kitchen

GRANNY LUV'S HUMMINGBIRD CAKE

Cake Ingredients:

3 cups all-purpose flour

2 cups granulated sugar

1 teaspoon salt

1 teaspoon baking soda

1 teaspoon ground
cinnamon

3 large eggs, beaten

1½ cups vegetable oil

1½ teaspoons vanilla extract

1 (8 ounce) can crushed
pineapple in juice

3 chopped ripe bananas

1 cup chopped pecans or
walnuts

Cream Cheese Frosting:

2 (8 ounce) packages
softened cream cheese

1 cup salted butter
(unsalted won't work)

2 (16 ounce) packages powdered sugar

2 teaspoons Madagascar vanilla
extract

Directions:

Bake cake layers:

Preheat oven to 350 degrees. Mix flour, sugar, salt, baking soda, and
cinnamon. Add eggs and oil until moistened. Stir in vanilla,

pineapple, bananas, and nuts. Divide evenly into three greased and floured 9-inch round cake pans. Bake 25 to 30 minutes until toothpick inserted in center comes out clean. Cool at least 10 minutes on a wire rack then remove to finish cooling completely (at least an hour).

Prepare cream cheese frosting:
Mix cream cheese and butter until smooth. Slowly add in powdered sugar until blended then stir in vanilla. Beat until fluffy.

Assemble cake:
Place cake layer on platter and spread with one cup frosting. Top with second cake layer and another cup frosting. Add third layer, frost entire cake, and arrange nuts on top. For added decoration, crushed nuts can be applied around edges.

Read on for a sneak peek of another exciting book in the Savannah Secrets series!

Season's Meetings

BY ANNE MARIE RODGERS

THE INTERVIEW, PART 1

Mason Denton
Grade 6
Effingham County Middle School
English Language Arts

My assignment: Interview a senior citizen with an interesting life story and write a transcript of the interview. (Transcript = a written or printed record of material originally presented in another way, such as an interview.)

Interview with my great-grandfather **Sumner Denton**, age 93, Guyton, GA, 10/12/2020.

Interviewer: *Great-Granddaddy, you showed me an old newspaper photo of you and your sisters and brother from when you were little. What did the newspaper photo say?*

SD: It said, "Five Children for Sale. Five children in rural Guyton, Georgia, will be sold or given away by their widowed mother, who can no longer care for them." A man from the newspaper came and took the picture. I had the newspaper for a long time, and I pestered the lady I worked for until she told me what it said. After I learned to read, I memorized it. Two little sentences. You wouldn't think two little sentences could say so much about somebody's life. Sometimes I looked at it, trying to fix everything I could in my mind about the others—my little sisters and brother.

Interviewer: How did you feel about getting sold?

SD: Well, I didn't really understand what was happening until after, when I was taken away, and it was years before I found out Mrs. Healy had paid money for me. But being taken away was pretty terrible. How could anybody sell their children? I remember the day my first child was born. I looked down at her little red, squished face and wondered how anyone could give their own child away. I know it's not my place to judge. Still, I wish, just once, I could go back in time and talk to my mama, ask her if it really was so bad that she had to sell us. Like we were furniture or something. But then, I guess it was, since she died little more'n a year later. Mrs. Healy, the lady I worked for, she said Mama was hysterical and she drowned. Mama didn't even know how to swim, and she would never have gone in the pond. I couldn't figure how she could have drowned. It wasn't until a lot of years had passed that I understood Mama had probably killed herself. I imagine she was pretty sad over my father's death and the fact that she couldn't provide for the five of us. That's probably what led to her selling us. And selling us off is probably what led her to kill herself. At least, that's how I see it. Makes it a little easier to forgive her, you know? She must have been one heartsick lady.

Interviewer: Great-Granddaddy, what do you remember about taking the picture?

SD: The newspaper photo? I remember the day it was taken, probably because that day was so different from every other day. First, Ma bathed all five of us, from me right down to the baby. Then she dressed us all in the least worn-out of our clothes. No shoes, because who had money for shoes during the Depression? She made us sit on the front porch so we wouldn't get dirty, and she gave me a piece of candy to break into five tiny little pieces so every kid could have one. I was in charge of making sure little Tillie didn't choke. She was barely a year old, and I was seven. What kind of job was that for a seven-year-old?

Mama was crying in the kitchen when the man came. I say kitchen, but we only had the two rooms. It wasn't much, but after Daddy died, we had to move out'n the place where we were before. That little shack was where Tillie was born, without a single grown-up female around to help. Just me'n Bobbie Dee and the two little ones.

Anyway, we looked at the man, and I called Mama, but none of us moved because Ma said she'd tan our hides if we got dirty. So, the man set up this long contraption on sticks and set his black picture box on top of it. We didn't know at the time it was a camera and a tripod, but I'll never forget it. He wanted Mama in the picture too, but she wouldn't. I don't remember the For Sale sign at all, but I couldn't read back then, because I never went to school till I was at Mrs. Healy's.

Interviewer: *Who was Mrs. Healy?*

SD: Mrs. Healy, she was a widow. She's the one who bought me. I went first. I didn't want to go, but she handed two dollars to Mama and told me, "Come on, boy," so I went. Didn't want the little kids to see me cry or carry on. Mama wouldn't even say goodbye or hug me or nothing. She just put her apron over her head and ran inside. I sort of understand that now, but down deep inside where that little kid lives, it still makes me hurt. I never saw my mama again.…